Seal Island

Seal Island

JULIA GREEN

Illustrated by Paul Howard

OXFORD
UNIVERSITY PRESS

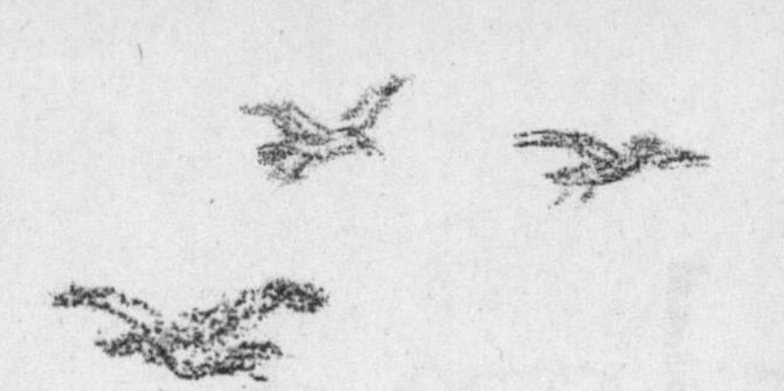

OXFORD
UNIVERSITY PRESS

Great Clarendon Street, Oxford OX2 6DP
Oxford University Press is a department of the University of Oxford.
It furthers the University's objective of excellence in research, scholarship,
and education by publishing worldwide in

Oxford New York

Auckland Cape Town Dar es Salaam Hong Kong Karachi
Kuala Lumpur Madrid Melbourne Mexico City Nairobi
New Delhi Shanghai Taipei Toronto

With offices in

Argentina Austria Brazil Chile Czech Republic France Greece
Guatemala Hungary Italy Japan Poland Portugal Singapore
South Korea Switzerland Thailand Turkey Ukraine Vietnam

First published 2014

British Library Cataloguing in Publication Data

Data available

ISBN: 978-0-19-273566-9
9 10 8

Printed in Great Britain
Paper used in the production of this book is a natural,
recyclable product made from wood grown in sustainable forests
The manufacturing process conforms to the environmental
regulations of the country of origin

For Alison
with love

Contents

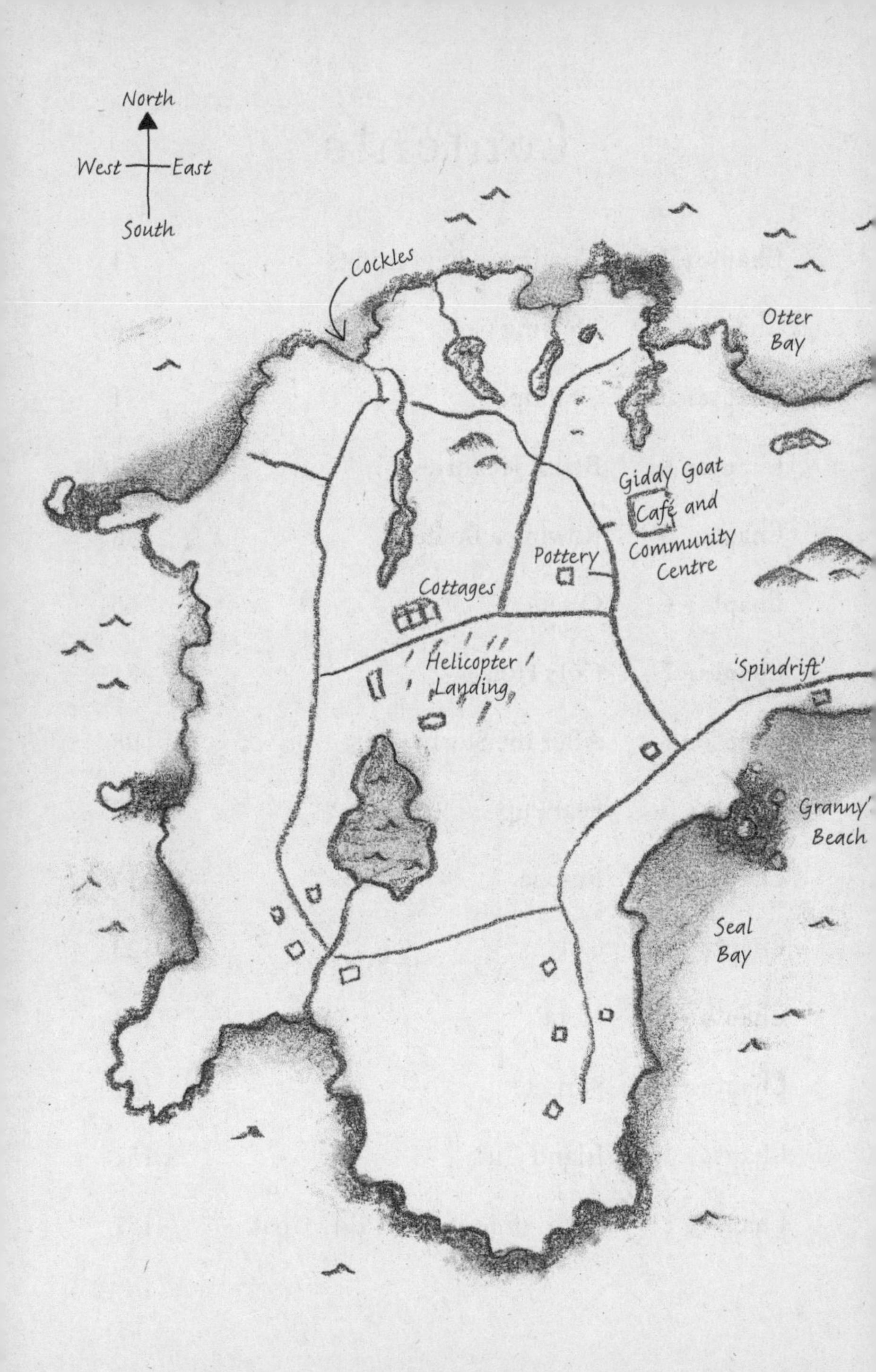
North
West
East
South
Cockles
Otter Bay
Giddy Goat Café and Community Centre
Pottery
Cottages
Helicopter Landing
'Spindrift'
Granny'
Beach
Seal Bay

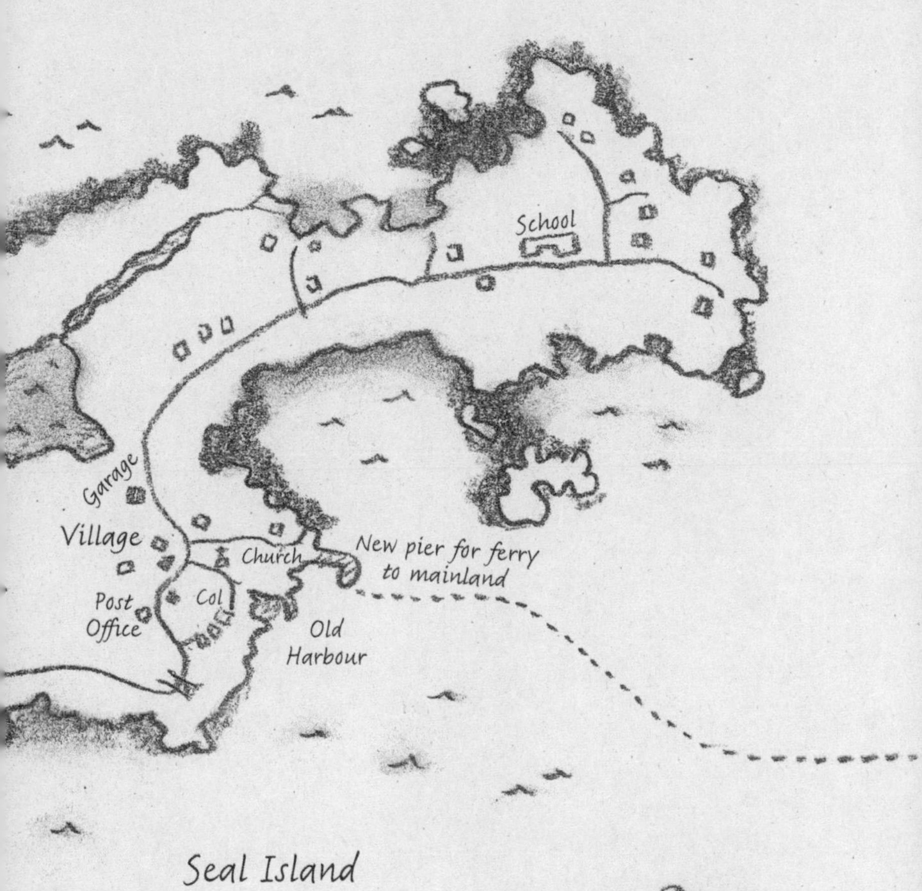
School
Garage
Village
Church
New pier for ferry
to mainland
Post
Office
Col
Old
Harbour
Seal Island

Uninhabited
Islands

Chapter 1

Goodbyes, Beginnings

Grace watched the ferry from the island pier, waiting for the moment when Mum and Dad would come up on the deck to wave goodbye to her. The ferrymen untied the mooring ropes, closed the big gates at the back of the car deck with a loud clang, and the ferry clanked and banged as it pulled away from the pier and chugged slowly out into the open sea.

There they were, standing by the railings at the back of the ferry. Mum and Dad each held one of the babies, and Kit stood between them, waving madly at Grace.

'Goodbye!' Grace called over and over, even though they probably couldn't hear her above the sound of the ferry engine.

Dad got his white handkerchief out of his pocket and waved it, like someone in an old-fashioned film, just like Grandpa used to do.

Grace watched and waved. This was the first time ever she'd stayed behind on the island with Granny. Bubbles of excitement fizzed in her tummy. All the things she was going to do . . . the adventures she was going to have without Kit tagging behind or babies to look after or Mum worrying . . .

They'd had a whole week together on the island, and now Mum, Dad, Kit, and the babies were travelling home. The ferry would take them to the mainland, where they'd catch the train south, to the city, and home, and normal life. While lucky Grace stayed here.

The ferry chugged further away, followed by its trail of screeching gulls. The white wake the ferry left behind was like a path across the water, stretching longer and thinner and fainter as it went further out to sea. Mum and Dad were just small dots, now, and she couldn't see Kit at all. Was that Dad's white handkerchief she could still see, flapping back and forth, a final goodbye? The ferry altered direction slightly, pulling hard against the current and the tide, and chugged on, faster than she'd expected. Soon it had disappeared from view completely.

After all the noise and activity of the big ferry, it seemed suddenly silent. For just a second, Grace felt utterly alone. And then that moment passed, and she noticed the wind ruffling the water as it slapped against the pier, and a flurry of small brown birds flying overhead, and she heard Granny calling her name.

'Grace? Ready to go back?'

Grace turned and ran up the slope towards the car park and the bench where Granny was waiting for her.

'What now?' Granny asked. 'An ice cream from the post office shop? Before we walk home?'

Grace nodded. The wind made her eyes sting. Her throat hurt from shouting *Goodbye*! so many times.

The car park was already empty. The wind blew tufts of white seed-fluff from the thistles growing along the edge. The lady at the ferry ticket office was locking the door of the kiosk. 'No more ferries till Saturday,' Granny said.

'So we're totally cut off?' Grace asked. 'That's exciting!'

Granny smiled. 'Well, I suppose you could put it like that. But there are all the fishing boats, of course. And the helicopter landing pad, for use in an emergency.'

'What kind of an emergency?' Grace asked.

'Well, if you broke your leg or something,' Granny said. 'But of course you won't do that.'

They walked along the road towards the village. Granny took Grace's hand for a moment and squeezed it tight. 'I always find it hard to see the family go,' she said. 'But it will be lovely with just the two of us. I don't know how your mum manages. Those babies are a handful!'

The wind was blowing stronger than ever. It blew Grace's hair so it tickled her face and got in her mouth. She scooped her hair back and tucked it into her collar. It was too hard to talk, facing into the wind, so they walked on side by side in silence. Sheep grazing on the open moorland either side of the road scattered, baaing, as they went past.

They reached the first houses in the village, and the church with its thick stone walls. They took the short-cut through the churchyard. Here, it was sheltered from the wind. They both breathed out and laughed.

'Phew, that's a relief!' Granny said. 'It's a battle, isn't it? The wind versus us.'

'We won,' Grace said. 'It didn't blow us into the sea or off the road into the bog.'

Grandpa's grave was close to the wall. Granny, Dad, and Grace had put a posy of wild flowers there yesterday and the small pink petals still looked fresh and bright. Granny fiddled around with the flowers in the jam jar, tidying them up a bit.

Grace left her to it. She walked round the church building to the other side so she could see the sea, one field away beyond the churchyard wall. Grey waves topped with white. Birds flew low across the bay. And someone or something else was out there, in the surf: a person in a wetsuit, or possibly a seal . . . it was too far away to be sure.

'Ready?' Granny called.

'Yes!' Grace ran back to join her. They battled against the wind all the way to the post office shop.

Grace pushed the door open and went to peer into the freezer cabinet. The ice creams were next to the frozen peas and fish fingers and there wasn't much choice.

'I'll have chocolate, please. Two scoops.'

Granny chose strawberry.

The grey-haired lady behind the counter laughed. 'It's not really an ice cream sort of day.' She scooped the ice cream into cones.

Granny explained they were celebrating. 'It's Grace's first holiday with me by herself, and we're going to have ice cream every day if we feel like it!'

'Lucky you. Anything else, Mairi? Any stamps or parcels today?' the lady asked Granny.

'That's all thank you, Flora,' Granny said.

Grace looked around the shop while Granny chatted to the lady. Flora: what an old-fashioned name. It matched the old-fashioned island post office, nothing like the one near Grace's home in the city. This one sold everything: groceries and cards and toys, newspapers and vegetables, bags of peat and firelighters, and cough medicine and wine. The post office bit of the shop was at one end of the wooden counter, with a glass partition. It reminded Grace of the toy post office set that had belonged to Mum when she was little, which she'd given to Grace when she was about five. It had a date stamp, an ink pad, some little envelopes and pretend money, and a toy till that made a lovely *ping* sound when you pressed the keys.

'Goodbye, Flora!' Granny was saying.

Grace quickly chose a postcard to send to her best friend, Molly. It had a seal's sweet face on the front. She paid the money and Flora put it in a paper bag for her.

Grace and Granny walked through the tiny village and out the other side, over the cattle grid. Grace was good at balancing on the grid, but Granny went through the gate at the side. They kept walking along the single-track road as it followed the curve of a big sandy bay. The wind was still blowing hard. It swept through the coarse grass on the dunes and made everything quiver and dance.

Ahead of them, Grace could see the white walls of Granny's house, right next to the beach. Grace licked her ice cream all the way round the cone, to catch all the drips. She finished the final chocolate-filled tip of the cone as they went through the gate into Granny's front yard.

But Grace wasn't ready to go inside. 'Can I go down on the beach, Granny?' she asked. 'There might be seals.'

'Of course,' Granny said. 'I'll start making the tea.'

Grace ran across the white sand. No one else was on the beach this afternoon. No sign of seals, either. Three big seagulls flew away and a whole flock of tiny pale brown birds took off together as she got to the edge of the sea, their wings flashing silver. Their thin reedy calls echoed over the sand. 'Come back!' Grace called to them. She tried to remember what they were called. Grandpa had tried to teach her the names of the seabirds.

The waves broke as they came over a reef of rocks out in the bay and spread like lace onto the sand. Grace pulled off her trainers and socks and paddled in the shallow water. She played a game of catch with the waves, running up the beach ahead of them. The water was icy. She danced all along the edge of the sea for a long way.

She stopped to look out at the reef again: something was there, watching her. She strained her eyes against the bright light. A seal was swimming just beyond the rocks. She blinked. Two seals, no, three: they were swimming together, playing in the surf. 'Hello seals!' Grace called. The wind snatched away the sound of her voice and mixed it with the crash of the waves.

Seals looked a bit like people when you saw them swimming, with their smooth heads, and the dark eyes. Seals were Grace's favourite animals. They were Granny's favourite too. Granny knew lots of stories about them. Island people said you could sometimes hear seals singing. And in the stories, sometimes they came onto the shore, and left their seal skins behind and became human, just for a while . . .

Grace bent down to pick up a pretty pebble: pink and grey, with sparkly bits. A wave splashed up her legs and soaked her jeans. Grace laughed. 'You win!' she told the sea.

She stood up. The wind tugged at her hair and pulled it free from where she'd tucked it in her collar. Her hands and feet were almost numb with cold. She watched the seals for a while longer. It looked as if they were having fun, surfing the waves just like people do.

Grace shivered. Time to go back for tea and to warm up. She called goodbye to the seals, even though they couldn't hear her. She skipped back along the sand to pick up her shoes and socks. She ran with bare feet back to Granny's house, climbed the wooden steps that led to the wooden decking at the back of the house and left her sandy trainers outside the door.

Granny was in the kitchen. 'Tea's nearly ready,' she said. 'You look cold! Do you want to make a fire in the peat stove, Grace? We might as well get cosy this evening.'

The peat came in hard dark-coloured bricks from the post office shop. In olden times, the people on the island would have dug the peat up with special spades and stacked it to dry, ready for burning on an open fire instead of wood or coal. Peat was rotted-down moss and grass and other plants, and you could still find it in the boggy ground all over the island.

Grace rolled sheets of old newspaper and tied them in loose twists, the way Granny did, to get the fire started. Next she laid the peat bricks, and adjusted the air vents on the cast iron stove. She crouched back on her heels to watch the flames catch and lick up the sides of the paper, and listened to the roar as the fire got hotter. It was satisfying, knowing how to make a proper fire.

Grace climbed up onto the window seat and looked out. She remembered what Dad had said about her stay on the island. *You'll be able to run and play as free and wild as a bird, just like Granny used to do when she was a child.*

The very best thing about Granny's house was how close it was to the beach. It was about as near to living on a beach as you could get, without living actually in a beach-hut or a sea-cave. When you opened the door, sand and bits of shell and dried seaweed drifted in. Before Granny and Grandpa had bought it, five years ago, the house had belonged to a fisherman, and he had left two rotten old lobster pots in the yard, and a length of torn fishing net, which Granny had woven into the fence as decoration. Grandpa had carved the name of the house on a piece of driftwood next to the front door: *Spindrift.*

Even when you were inside, it still felt as if you were part of the beach. You could hear the sea, especially on stormy days when the waves pounded the rocks. At night it lulled you to sleep with its steady shushing sound.

Grace peered out: what were the seals doing now? She picked up the binoculars that Granny kept by the window for watching the birds. They were big and heavy and it was hard to make them focus. There! One seal was still playing in the surf. With the binoculars, Grace could actually see its mottled cream-and-grey skin, and its big dark eyes. Even though she knew it was impossible, it looked as if the seal was smiling straight back at her.

After tea, Grace looked at Granny's book about island wildlife. She read what it said about seals. There were two kinds up here in the Hebrides: grey seals and harbour, or common, seals. The ones she'd been watching in the bay were harbour seals, with more rounded faces. The grey seals had pups in the autumn, but harbour seal pups were born in the summer, in June and July. Grace's heart beat a bit faster. Imagine that! Baby seals! Perhaps she'd actually see a real baby seal this week.

She went to find the postcard she'd bought at the shop for Molly, and wrote:

Dear Molly,

Hope you are having a nice holiday. Today I saw seals, like this one. I might get to see a baby one! The beach is amazing but today was too cold to swim. Granny's house is right next to the beach. Love Grace x x x

Grace got out her new sketchbook and water-colour paints, a holiday present from Dad. She fetched a cup of water from the kitchen and set it down on the window seat beside her. She opened the sketchbook and smoothed her hand across the thick creamy paper. Carefully, she dipped her brush in the water and painted the first line of blue. The watery paint spread over the paper just like sea. She mixed brown, and a tiny bit of black and white and a dash of yellow, and painted the shape of the seal, its head bobbing above the water and the rest of it beneath the sea.

Granny sat down on the sofa and put her feet up. Grace showed her the painting.

'It's lovely,' Granny said. 'You've captured the light on the sea beautifully, and the seal's whiskery face. You can send it to Mum and Dad, like a home-made postcard.'

'I'm going to paint something every day,' Grace told Granny. 'Like a diary, but in pictures. One special thing for each day, to remember it for ever.'

'That's a good idea,' Granny said. 'Now, it's time for your shower and bed. It's getting late, even though it's still so light outside. The island is so far north it hardly gets dark at all this time of year.'

Grace spoke to Mum and Dad on the phone before she got into bed. They'd reached the mainland and were staying in a hotel for the night. Tomorrow they'd catch the train home.

'Are you missing us?' Mum asked.

Grace could hear Kit grumbling in the background, and the babies squawking. 'Not really,' she said. 'Are you missing me?'

Mum laughed. 'Of course, Grace! But I'm very happy you're having a lovely time. Now, sleep tight.'

'Mind the bed bugs don't bite!' Dad shouted, loud enough for Grace to hear.

Grace laughed. She gave the phone back to Granny, and snuggled down under the covers. The sea was roaring outside: it must be high tide. She imagined the seals, still swimming in the dark. Or maybe they were hauled out on the rocks by now, sleeping.

She yawned. Already she was drifting . . . nearly asleep herself.

Chapter 2

Meeting Col

Grace lay in bed, snug and warm, listening to the early morning sounds in Granny's house. Granny was pottering about: Grace heard the click as she switched on the kettle, and the soft sweep of the broom as Granny brushed up the sand in the hallway. She heard the rattle of the peat stove as Granny cleared out the ash from the fire, the squeak of the cupboard doors as Granny opened them to get out bowls and plates and laid the table for breakfast.

Grace smiled. She loved all these noises, and what they meant. It was very different from her real home, where mornings were always a rush and no one had time to sit round the breakfast table and all Mum's attention was on spooning breakfast into the babies' mouths and stopping them dropping food onto the floor and making a lunch box for Kit and telling Grace to *hurry up*.

Granny could take all the time she wanted now she no longer had to go out to work. She liked the days to have a pattern: tidying up and cleaning every morning. 'A place for everything, and everything in its place,' she said. Once all the jobs had been done, the day was theirs to do whatever they chose.

Grace climbed out of bed and drew back the curtains. A sunny morning! Good. She got dressed, ran downstairs and straight to the back door. She opened it wide. The tide was low: the big sandy beach lay before her, glistening in the early morning sunshine.

'Grace?' Granny called. 'Breakfast first!'

Oh, but it looked so tempting. 'Just one run down to the water and then I'll come back for breakfast. Please?'

Granny laughed. 'You're just like I used to be at your age. Go on then. I'll start making the porridge.'

Grace clattered down the wooden steps onto the beach. A flock of black and white birds flew off as she raced across the damp sand. They made a lovely sound with their piping calls and the flap of wings. She splashed through pools the sea had left behind. She picked up a pretty shell with pale pink stripes and another one curled tight like a snail. Closer to the water, there was a breeze that blew her hair back from her face, but playfully, not like yesterday's cold wind. The sea was deep blue all the way to the horizon, and the sky was a lighter shade of blue.

Someone else was up this early too. A boy with messy dark hair and a blue jacket and rolled-up jeans was running along next to the sea, dodging the waves that whooshed up the sand. Grace laughed as he misjudged a wave and water splashed up his legs and soaked his jeans.

The boy looked up and grinned at her as she got nearer. 'Hello!' he called.

'Hello!' Grace called back. She slowed down and stopped next to him.

The boy smiled. 'You're Grace,' he stated. It wasn't a question.

'Yes. How did you know?'

'My nan said you were staying. She knows your nan.'

'Granny.'

The boy looked at Grace. His eyes were blue, the same deep sparkly colour as the sea. 'Nan, Gran, it's the same thing. I'm Col. Did you see the sanderlings?'

Grace shook her head. 'What are they?'

'Those funny little wading birds that look like wind-up clockwork toys, the way they run. And the black and white birds with red legs are oyster catchers.'

Grace hadn't ever met a boy her age who knew the names of birds. But then, there weren't many birds where she lived. Blackbirds and magpies and pigeons and starlings: that was about it.

'Do you live here all the time?' Grace asked him.

'Yes. Our house is in that row by the old harbour. Dad's a fisherman.'

'What sort of fish?'

'Lobsters, mostly. Crabs. Scallops. Shellfish.'

Grace didn't know what scallops were. She could look it up in that book at Granny's. 'I saw seals, yesterday,' she said.

The boy smiled. 'Grey or harbour?'

'Harbour seals,' Grace said. She felt pleased that she knew the difference.

Col didn't look like someone who would laugh at her and make her feel stupid. 'Have you seen baby seals?' she asked him. 'Do you know where I could find them?'

'Not here,' Col said. 'Seals haul up to have their pups on the rocks offshore. Or the uninhabited islands, like Mingulay. But harbour seal pups can swim almost straightaway, so you might see them swimming in the bay, if you're lucky. Now's about the right time of year.'

Grace could see Granny on the deck, waving at her to come in for breakfast.

'I've got to go now,' Grace said.

'OK. See you again.'

Grace nodded. 'Bye.' She ran up the beach. She turned once to wave, but Col was already running on, dodging the waves, intent on his game with the sea.

'I met a boy called Col,' she told Granny while they ate their breakfast. 'And he already knew my name.'

'He's an island boy, that's why.' Granny laughed. 'Everyone knows everyone else on this island. All the comings and goings. Col is Flora's grandson. He's about your age.'

'Has he got any sisters?'

'No. There's just him, his little brother Benny, and baby Lewis. He's the eldest in the family, like you.'

Grace thought about that. At school, all her real friends were girls. There were boys, of course, but she didn't really have anything to do with them. Not anymore. It was different when they were all younger. Something had changed this year. Now, the girls sat about in one corner of the playground at break-times, and the boys mostly rushed around in the rest of the space. Still, she wasn't at school now. Here, she could do whatever she liked. She could be friends with a boy if she wanted to.

'I've got cakes to bake this morning for the Giddy Goat community café,' Granny said. 'Do you want to help?' She took a scrap of paper down from behind the magnet on the fridge door. 'Cup cakes with icing, and flapjacks, and a couple of rounds of ginger biscuits are on my list for today,' she said. 'You could do the icing, Grace.'

'I'd like to go back to the beach, first,' Grace said. 'But I'll help you later, Granny.'

'Lovely,' Granny said. 'Please stay where I can see you from the house, and be back by lunchtime. Don't go in the sea without telling me, will you?'

'I won't be swimming,' Grace said. 'It's too cold. I'll be beachcombing. And looking out for seals, of course.' It felt strange at first, doing whatever she felt like. Always before, Kit had been with her on the beach, tugging her hand, wanting her to dam a stream with him or pretend to be a killer whale or play sharks, asking questions all the time and not listening to her answers. And Mum would be worrying about the babies eating sand or keeping their sunhats on or whether they needed a nap. Today, Grace could choose to do exactly what she wanted. How amazing was that!

The beach was deserted again. There was no sign of Col. The sand gleamed white in the sun. Grace did a cartwheel, and then two more, to practise. The third one was almost as good as the ones Hattie Cross did at school. It was much easier doing cartwheels here on the beach when no one was looking and judging her.

There was nothing like a perfect cartwheel for making you feel totally free and happy.

She went along the high tide line next, to see what she could find. Tiny flies buzzed up from the seaweed as she kicked it. She found a length of blue string, and a perfect creamy-white shell. Further along, she picked up a piece of driftwood, bleached pale by the waves. It looked a bit like a boat already. She could add a mast and float it on one of the rock pools at the edge of the bay. She put it in her pocket and went on searching for a suitable stick to make the mast. She needed a knife, really. A penknife like the one Grandpa used to keep in his pocket, with different blades and a bottle opener and all sorts of other gadgets: even a tiny pencil.

Where was it now?

She didn't want to think about that. She did some more cartwheels instead. Whoops! The piece of driftwood and all the pebbles and shells plopped out of her pockets and scattered over the sand. She ran back to gather them up.

How good it felt to run on an empty beach! She ran all the way to the rocks, and then stopped to check Granny could still see her from the window, since she'd promised. Just about, she reckoned, if Granny used the binoculars. Anyway, she was perfectly safe. She climbed up the stack of rocks and found an enormous rock pool. If she kept her shadow off the water, she could watch a whole other world going about its daily business. Red anemone blobs stuck to the sides waved their fronds under the water as if they were stroking it. Shrimps darted backwards. Tiny striped fish skittered about and down under an edge of rock a crab lurked, waiting. The seaweed was all different colours, like you'd never expect: pink and silver and bright green and gold. It was an underwater forest, weird and magical. The more she looked, the more she saw. She knew each high tide brought a new pattern of pools, refreshed and changed the water, and brought new creatures. Nothing stays the same for long on a beach.

Grace tucked her hair back behind her ears to keep it out of her eyes. Right at the bottom of the pool a beautiful shiny shell gleamed and glittered. She pushed her sleeve up and reached down. The water was deeper than she expected and her sleeve got wet. She examined the shell she'd fished up. The outside was pale cream but the inside shone like pearl and in the sunlight it flashed a whole rainbow of colours. She put it safely in her pocket with the other shells.

Grace clambered over the slippery rocks near the sea. There weren't so many pools here, but the rocks themselves were shaggy with slimy green weed and dotted with the red and purple blobs of sea-anemones. Other rocks were crusty with barnacles and the bigger shells of limpets. Grace found a nearly dry patch of rock and sat there in the sun, her legs dangling down over the water below. She was perfectly happy just sitting there for a long time. She watched the light dancing on the water, and held up her face to feel the warm sun.

Something else was moving through the water. Grace held her breath as she watched. It wasn't a seabird or a bit of floating driftwood. It was too big to be a fish. Now she could make out the mottled, sand-coloured body, sleek in the water. It swam closer and raised its head to look right at her: the round smooth face of a seal, with big dark eyes and whiskers. It stayed there, watching, as if it was checking her out and seeing if she was a danger. Grace sat still and quiet. The seal dived and swooped under the surface; it played and tumbled in the breaking waves as if it was a surfer. Grace laughed, and the seal's head popped up again, listening.

Grace remembered Granny telling her how seals liked music, how they would come to listen if you sang. Grace checked there was no one else around: no, she was still the only person on the entire beach. She sang a verse of a song from school, simply because it was the first thing that came into her head. Her voice rang out clear and true and the seal stayed there, listening. She sang louder.

'There's a time to laugh,
there's a time to cry,
a time for birth when you say hello,
a time to turn and wave goodbye . . .'

And then suddenly she had to stop because she had a lump in her throat and her eyes were prickling with tears. She hugged her knees to herself. The seal dived down again. She watched it swim, effortless and agile, dipping and turning, and then it dived again and she couldn't see it any more.

It kept happening: the sudden tightening of her throat and tears in her eyes.

Grandpa . . .

. . . the memories were flooding back, because he was everywhere in this place; even small things like the penknife would set her off again, and now the words of the song had done it. *Goodbye . . .*

Grace stood up and shivered. She waited a little longer to see if the seal would reappear, but it had swum away into deeper water.

The tide had gone down since she'd arrived: now, she could simply slip down off the end of the rocks onto the wet sand below and paddle round the outcrop, back to the main part of the beach. A family was making camp with striped windbreaks at the other end, and three small children in wetsuits were running in and out of the shallow water. Grace wondered what Kit and the babies were doing right now. She would ask Granny if she could phone later, to talk to them all again.

Grace ran in a zig-zag back up the beach towards the white house. Granny waved from the window as she got closer.

The kitchen was warm and smelt of baking.

'You can scrape out the mixing bowl, if you like,' Granny said. 'It's all buttery and sweet.'

Grace spread her treasures out along the kitchen table to show Granny. 'This one's going to be a boat.' She pointed to the driftwood. 'I need a knife, to shape a hull.'

'I like the mother-of-pearl shell,' Granny said. She turned it over in her hand. For a few seconds she was quiet, staring through the window. 'If you look in the top drawer in the wooden chest you will find the tools your grandpa used for making things. You could use them to make your boat, if you like.'

Granny turned back to Grace. 'Now, put your beachcombings somewhere else and we can make the cake icing together. Wash your hands and shake the sand off yourself first, though. You look as if you've been rolling in it!'

Grace arranged the shells and pretty pebbles along

the top of the bookcase in her bedroom, next to the row of little wooden boats that Grandpa had carved a long time ago when she was small. Each one was different. She washed her hands in the little bathroom with its sea horse shower curtain. Her fingers still sparkled with sand: little shiny grains of mica that stuck to the skin.

She went back into the kitchen. She helped Granny make icing with sugar and a tiny bit of water and colouring: the palest pink, sea blue, and buttercup yellow. They took it in turns to spread the icing on the top of the little sponge cakes and add decorations: silver balls, multi-coloured hundreds and thousands, or a tiny piece of red glacé cherry.

'We'd better try one,' Granny said. 'Just to be sure they taste as good as they look.' She filled the kettle and got the cups out for coffee for her and hot chocolate for Grace.

Grace chose a cake with pale blue icing and silver sprinkles. 'This is the prettiest,' she told Granny, 'and it tastes delicious.'

Granny started washing up the mixing bowls.

'Shall I help?' Grace asked.

'It will only take me a minute,' Granny said. 'Why don't you find those tools and make your boat? I want you to have some fun, Grace. You did more than your fair share of helping when Kit and the babies were here.'

Grace lingered a moment longer. 'I saw a seal,' she said. 'I sang to it.'

Granny smiled.

'It's funny without Grandpa here,' Grace said.

Granny stopped washing the dishes for a moment. She stared straight ahead, out of the window at the sea. 'Yes. We both miss him terribly,' she said. 'But we have to get used to it. And Grandpa would want us to have fun. He'd be very happy, knowing you were going to carve your own wooden boat.'

Grace nodded. 'I'll make the very best boat I can. For Grandpa.'

Chapter 3

★

Grandpa

Grace picked up her piece of driftwood and went to look in the wooden chest. It stood in the corner of the conservatory on the south-west side of the house. The sun through the glass made it warm in here, and brought out the smell of the lemon-scented geraniums in the pots along the windowsill.

Grace pulled open the top drawer and immediately the smell of Grandpa flooded out: like wood-shavings, and glue, and something else she couldn't describe: the smell of a woollen jumper when you hug it close, mixed with pepper and whisky and peat smoke.

The red penknife was there, on top of some sheets

of sandpaper. She took it out, carefully looked at the different blades and gadgets. She chose the middle-sized blade and trimmed the edges of the driftwood, shaving off pieces to make it like the hull of a boat. Grandpa had taught her how to cut carefully, away from yourself, so you didn't slip and cut your hand by mistake. She worked slowly, carefully, and a small pile of curled wood-shavings collected in her lap. She stood up to get a piece of sandpaper, to smooth the edges, and the shavings tipped onto the floor.

Granny watched from the open doorway. 'You found what you needed?'

Grace nodded. She ran her finger around the wooden hull. The wood was smooth and soft as silk. Next she made a small hole for the mast, a snug fit for the stick she'd found on the beach. 'It's not as good as Grandpa's boats,' she said.

'Grandpa had years of practice,' Granny said. 'That's how you get to be good at something. Yours is very good, for a first boat. It's original and unique. You found a good piece of driftwood. I wonder what it came from? A tea-chest perhaps, on board a ship on a long voyage across the ocean from Africa or India and there was a big storm and it got washed overboard . . .' Granny was off again, making up stories.

Grace half-listened. She was thinking about the little boat. Did it need a sail, perhaps? A triangle of cloth, stitched to the mast . . . She would look in Granny's sewing basket, later, for a spare scrap of white cotton.

'After lunch,' Granny said, 'I'm taking the cakes over to the café. Do you want to come?'

Grace nodded. 'And later, I'm going to sail my boat.'

'You should give it a name,' Granny said.

'Like what?' Grace asked.

'I don't know. It will come to you,' Granny said. 'Just give it time.'

It was a long walk to the café. Granny didn't have a car on the island. She usually went by bike, with the cakes and biscuits in tins in a basket hooked over the handlebars, but today they walked the whole way. The road wound round the edge of the island, and then branched off, across the island, past the pottery and to the Giddy Goat café and community centre.

Grace opened the door for Granny.

A big man with curly grey hair and a bushy beard was wiping down tables and taking trays back to the kitchen. 'Fresh supplies? Good. We've had a run on cakes this morning.'

'Hello Angus.' Granny put the cake tins down on the counter. She said hello to a couple eating soup at one of the window tables, and they chatted for a while about the weather and the island news. 'This is my eldest granddaughter, Grace,' she told them.

'Hello Grace,' the man said. 'You here for your holidays? You'll have a whale of a time.' He laughed at his own joke. 'Whales. Minke. Orca. You see them round here sometimes. Get it?'

It wasn't a very good joke, Grace thought.

While Granny chatted some more, Grace went off to look at the exhibition in the community centre next to the café. There were posters about island life, the birds and insects and flowers that were rare and needed to be taken care of. There was a special rare kind of bee called a great yellow bumble bee. She looked at the photos of whales that swam near the island on their migration routes and another poster about seals. It said what to do if you found a stranded seal. There was a big photo of a harbour seal pup, staring out at her with its eyes like dark pools. Grace wondered what it would feel like to stroke its silky skin. Would it be warm and soft, like fur? Or smooth and cool, like a fish? There was a photograph of fishing boats, and something about problems with seals taking fish from the nets. Grace read the poster about life in a rock pool. Those red blobby anemones she'd seen were called 'Beadlet Anemones', and they were creatures, not plants!

Granny called from the doorway. 'Time to go, Grace.'

On the walk back, Granny chatted to Grace about what it was like, growing up as a child on the island and coming back to live here, now she was old. 'Well, not that old,' she said. I've got years of wonderful life ahead! Touch wood.' She reached her hand out to touch a wooden fence post.

Grace thought of Grandpa. He'd not been much older than Granny, and he'd died last year. But she didn't say that out loud.

'When I was little, everything here was dependent on the weather and the tides,' Granny said. 'Almost everyone scratched a living from the sea, and it was hard to make ends meet. But I was lucky: my mother was a midwife, so we had a regular income.'

'What's a midwife?' Grace asked.

'She helps women have their babies,' Granny said. 'Looks after the pregnant ones, and assists with the birth and then visits for a few days afterwards, to help the new mum with the baby. It was an important job. Most of the island women gave birth at home.'

Grace had seen the house where Granny had lived as a child, on the eastern side of the island. It had been extended and smartened up by the people who owned it now and rented it out as a holiday house.

'Why did you leave the island?' Grace asked.

'Well, I wanted to spread my wings and see the world,' Granny said. 'I went south, to university, and I met your grandpa and that was that. But you can't take the island out of the girl. I missed the sea like mad. I missed the big skies, and the call of the birds, and the space.'

They were almost back. Granny's house, perched on the edge of the bay, was like a beacon: the sun reflected off the windows and made them shine out. Grace ran ahead.

She pushed the door open. No one locked their doors on the island. There was no need to. Grace thought about home: the rush of traffic, the sirens

and car alarms going off at night. Here, there was the sound of wind and sea and birds, and that was all.

She found her wooden boat where she'd left it in the conservatory. She took it with her, and ran down onto the sand. There were three families camped out along the top of the beach, with windbreaks and blankets and deckchairs and beach stuff: it made it look crowded, even though Grace knew that was silly, when there was so much space really.

She ran in the other direction, towards the rock pools.

In the time she'd been away at the café, the tide had gone further out. The sun had warmed and dried the rocks; the rock pools shone like glass in the afternoon light. Grace jumped from one rock to the next, searching for the biggest pool. She knelt down and carefully placed the boat on the water. It seemed to float for a second, wobbled, and tipped over. She reached over to fish it out. She tried again, but this time it tipped over straightaway and floated on its side.

She frowned. What was wrong with it? Even a flat piece of wood would float. Perhaps the mast was too heavy and was overbalancing it?

A shadow fell over the pool. Grace looked up. The boy was there. She wondered how long he'd been watching her. She hadn't seen him coming along the beach.

Col smiled at her. 'Your boat needs a keel,' he said.

'What's that?' Grace said crossly.

'It balances the boat underneath. Like on a real boat. A small piece of slate would work. I'll find you some.' He jumped over the rocks, down onto the sand, and ran along the tideline. Grace saw him bend down to pick something up.

'Shall I show you how to do it?' he asked when he had climbed back up to join her. He held out his hand for the boat and Grace gave it to him. She watched him carefully slide the thin edge of slate into the bottom of her boat.

'Try it now,' Col said.

Grace took the boat from him and set it on the water. This time, it wobbled, and steadied, and then as the breeze rippled the surface of the pool, the little boat moved across the water. She watched it pick up speed, and then bump into the rocks the other side.

'Oh! It's perfect! Thank you,' she said. She was sorry she'd felt cross with him earlier, for interfering. She went round the pool and pushed the boat off the rocks so it could move freely again.

'It's a good little boat,' Col said. 'I could bring one of mine down, and we could race them.'

'All right,' Grace said shyly. 'But you'd win. Mine's just a home-made one.'

Col laughed. 'Mine too. And yours is just as good! Maybe better, if you made it a sail. We'll have to find a bigger pool, though. Seal Bay, the next one along, is better for rock pools. I'll see you there tomorrow, if you want?'

Grace nodded. 'OK. Yes please.'

'At low tide,' Col said. 'If my dad doesn't need me, that is. Now I've got to go home and help make tea.'

Grace watched him jog back along the sand. He ran in a kind of zig-zag, as if he was playing a game with himself. It made her smile. Col was nice, she thought. Friendly and natural; not showing off. He just assumed Grace would want to do the same things as him. Not at all like the boys at school.

She studied her boat as it floated on the rock pool. A sail would help catch the wind and make it go faster.

She'd make one tonight with Granny.

The tide was on its way in now. It came in fast: the waves looping up the flat sand. Every seventh wave seemed bigger than the rest. She counted the waves in, and most times it worked like that: six smaller waves and a seventh big one. Further along the beach, the families were packing up their things. The rock where she was sitting would be completely underwater in an hour or so, and all the rock pools would be flooded and part of the proper sea again. The sea had already reached the end of the rocky outcrop, splashing up spray.

Her face was glowing from a whole day of sun. She'd not noticed before. She rolled up her leggings and paddled back through the shallow waves to Granny's house, her boat tucked under her arm.

Chapter 4

Bedtime Stories

Grace lay in her bed, waiting for Granny to come and tell her stories. She thought back over the day: how simple and easy and fun it had been. She'd seen her seal, close up, made a boat like Grandpa's, and made friends with Col. Her painting that evening had been of the wooden boat with its new sail.

Her face and her arms still glowed from the sun. The hot water from her bath had made her skin pinker than ever.

'Sun-kissed skin,' Granny said when she came into the bedroom. 'You'll be as brown as a berry by the end of two weeks.'

'Berries aren't brown,' Grace said. 'They're red or pink or purple!'

'It's just a saying.' Granny sat down on the end of Grace's bed. 'Have you had a good day today?'

'Yes. Perfect.'

'Not missing your mum and dad too much?'

'Of course not!' Grace said. 'I'm ten, Granny!'

'Well, I'm sixty-five and I still miss them!' Granny said.

Grace laughed. 'Will you tell me a story? Please?'

'Are you sure you're not too grown-up for a bedtime story? A great girl of ten!' Granny teased.

At home, Grace always read to herself. No one had time to read to her, in any case. At bedtime, Mum would be tucking up the twins and singing to them while Dad helped Kit to settle down, or they'd be washing up or Dad would have papers to do for work. But Granny's bedtime stories were part of the fun of staying here. They were usually about the island; myths and legends, strange fairy tales and ghost stories that made Grace shiver deliciously.

She wriggled down under the duvet and waited while Granny made herself comfortable and decided which story to tell.

'Once upon a time, there was a fisherman,' Granny started. 'He was young and handsome and he lived alone in his white cottage by the beach.'

'Why did he live alone?' Grace asked.

'Because there were so few people on the island, and he hadn't found his one true love, yet,' Granny said.

'Go on,' Grace said.

'The fisherman was walking along the beach late one night under the moonlight, when he found a beautiful furry seal-skin, a mottled silvery-grey colour, draped over the damp pebbles. He picked it up. It was the most beautiful thing he had ever seen,

and so soft to stroke. He heard someone crying, and when he looked round, there was a beautiful young woman standing there.

'"Please give me back my seal-skin," she pleaded, "so I can return to my home and my family under the sea."

'The young man understood at once that she was a Selkie. Half woman, half seal. All the islanders knew about the Selkie people, although few had seen them. But the young man had already fallen in love with the beautiful young woman. He persuaded her to go with him back to his cottage. And he hid her seal-skin away so she would have to stay with him on land for ever . . .'

Grace's eyes were closing. Granny's voice murmured on, but Grace was no longer listening, she was so nearly asleep.

She woke up once, in the middle of the night. The room was pitch-dark. She had been dreaming about a seal girl, with a soft grey furry skin. Grace reached out to pull the curtains apart, and the room turned a silvery grey in the light of a shining moon.

She sat on the edge of the bed so she could see outside properly. The moon made a path of silver across the sea and glistened on the wet sand. The tide was still quite high. Small waves shushed in and out, calm and peaceful. For a second, she was so full of the dream that she could almost imagine she could see the strange figure of the seal girl, stepping through the shallow water and then beginning to swim out to another girl with dark hair who bobbed in the deeper water.

Grace stared. There was something there, she was sure of it. A dark shape, and then another. Was she still dreaming? She blinked, and when she looked again, she saw that it was two seals, bobbing and swimming in the breaking surf, as if they were playing under the starry moonlit sky.

Grace yawned. Now, she remembered the story Granny had been telling her as she drifted off to sleep. She didn't know what happened to the Selkie girl, because Granny hadn't finished telling the story.

She climbed back under the duvet and lay still, watching the moonlight make shadows round the room. It lit up the little boat, now perched on the dresser with its new white cotton sail, and it glinted on the glass of water by her bed, and it shone on the row of pebbles and shells along the top of the bookcase. The mother-of-pearl shell gleamed softly in the moonlight. She lay there, soothed by the rhythm of the waves on the shore, and the deep sense of peace all around. And then she must have slept, because suddenly it was morning.

Chapter 5

Rowing a Boat

It was the sun shining directly into her room now, not the moon. It was another perfect sunny morning. Grace tumbled out of bed and downstairs. The back door was wide open and Grace ran straight outside.

Granny was sitting on a chair reading in the sun, her cup of tea on the table beside her. She looked at Grace. 'You're late up this morning! Did you sleep well? You've missed Col: he came by to say hello. He has to help his dad later today but he asked if you wanted to go out fishing in the rowing boat with him first.'

'Can I?' Grace asked. 'Please?'

'Yes, if you wear a life jacket at all times, and stay

close to the shore. Do exactly what Col tells you: he has lots of experience. It's part of island life, knowing how to manage a boat. When I was a child, we all did.' Granny looked wistful. She smiled at Grace. 'We'll have breakfast outside in the sun, and then you can run along to Col's house.'

After breakfast, Grace walked along the beach road towards the village, holding the map Granny had drawn her. She checked it again. Over the cattle-grid, past the telecom masts and the public toilets, then a right turn downhill towards the old harbour, and Col's house was the one with the blue door in the middle of the row of houses.

How exciting, Grace thought, to be walking by herself. She almost never went anywhere by herself at home. Mum drove her to school, or to Molly's house, or the shops or the swimming pool. It was too far to walk and the roads were too busy and dangerous for her to ride a bike. This was exactly what Dad had meant, when he said Grace would be free as a bird on Granny's island . . .

Not a single car passed her on the beach road. A few sheep ran baaing out of her way, and some tiny brown birds flew up in a flurry. Up ahead, a post van was parked in front of the shop, but other than that the village looked deserted. She took the turning to the right. Ahead of her now was the old harbour, with three fishing boats moored up. One of them must belong to Col's dad. On her left, she saw the boarded-up hotel building—Granny said it had closed last summer—and the row of houses.

There! The blue door. It was slightly ajar, and Grace heard voices coming from inside. She hesitated. A child was crying, and a woman shouted something. Should she knock? Ring a bell? But she couldn't see a bell, and when she knocked with her hand it sounded feeble and she knew no one would hear her. She'd have to push the door open and go inside.

The door opened straight into a front room with a wooden floor and an old rag rug, a saggy sofa and two armchairs. A baby buggy was parked in one corner, and a basket of washing had been dumped in the middle of the floor. 'Hello? Col?' she called. 'It's me, Grace!'

The shouting stopped. A tired-looking woman came down the stairs. 'Oh,' she said. 'Sorry about all the noise! Col's out. He's getting the boat ready. You must be Mairi's granddaughter.' She held out her hand. 'Kate. Col's mum. Pleased to meet you.'

'Hello! I'm Grace.' She shook hands, since that seemed to be the right thing to do. 'Where will I find Col?' she asked.

'The boat shed's right by the beach. He's expecting you,' Col's mum—Kate—said.

A small boy appeared at the top of the stairs, half-hiding behind a square of blanket. Grace smiled at him. 'Hello!' she said. The boy stared at her but he didn't say anything. He was about three, Grace thought. She made a funny face, like she did sometimes to make the babies laugh when they played peekaboo with her.

The boy came slowly down the stairs, sucking his thumb and stroking the blanket, putting both feet on each step at a time. His mum picked him up and he nestled his head into her shoulder. 'Benny's a bit shy,' she said.

Grace knew that feeling. 'Well, I'll maybe see you later!' she said. 'Bye.' She went back out into the sunny lane.

And there was Col, down on the pebbly harbour beach, putting two oars into a small wooden rowing boat. She waved, and ran down to join him.

'All set?' Col said.

'Yes! It's so exciting! But I've got to wear a life jacket, Granny says.'

Col nodded. 'There's a spare one there for you.' He showed her how to put it on.

'Now you're here you can help me carry the boat down to the water. Have you rowed before?'

Grace shook her head. 'You can teach me.'

There was something magical about being in a small boat so close to the water, Grace thought. She had a small moment of panic, getting in, when she thought she'd tip and overbalance the boat, but she was fine. And now Col was rowing them out; the water this side of the harbour wall was smooth as silk. She could see down all the way to the seabed. She trailed a hand over the side: the water was freezing.

'You *can* swim?' Col asked.

'Yes, of course.'

'And you know that if something happens and we

capsize, it's safest to stay close to the boat? Hold onto it, if you can. Don't try to swim back to shore. It's always further than it looks.'

Grace nodded. She didn't tell Col that she was a brilliant swimmer, the best in her class. She had medals and certificates and everything. But it would sound as if she was showing off if she told him that. Instead, she carefully watched the way Col held the oars, how to lift and dip and turn them.

'Want to try?' he asked. 'You'll need to swap places with me.'

She moved forwards carefully, to sit beside Col. The boat wobbled alarmingly and Col laughed. To begin with, she took one oar and they rowed together, then she had a go with both oars. It was harder than it looked, to get the angle right so that both dipped at the same time and the same depth. And strange, to have your back to the direction you were heading. Her arms began to ache.

'OK. We'll go and find the place to fish, now. I'll take the oars, in case it's a bit choppy when the wind hits us,' Col said. They swapped places again.

Close up, the harbour wall seemed huge and frightening, and the boat seemed very small. It bobbed and

dipped on the waves at the harbour entrance, and Grace held on tight to the sides. Then they were through, out on the open sea where the waves were bigger, but she soon got used to the rocking movement. Col's confidence made her feel safe. He'd done this hundreds of times. Two fishermen mending nets on the harbour wall waved at them and Grace waved back.

'Look! A seal!' Grace pointed. A round dark head appeared and disappeared again a few metres ahead of them. 'It's watching us!'

Col didn't say anything. Maybe he'd seen so many they didn't seem special and exciting anymore. Grace thought about the night: the seals playing in the sea under the moon and how magical it had looked. She remembered the Selkie story. She wondered how it ended.

'They do look quite like people, don't they?' she said. 'With their big eyes and round heads.'

Col shrugged. 'Maybe. More like dogs, close up.'

The seal wasn't afraid of them, even though they were so near. Grace wished she could reach out her hand and touch its head. Col stopped rowing for a moment, resting the oars. The boat bobbed and danced on the moving water, tugged by the tide. The seal dived down again and swam away. The sunlight sparkled on the sea, blindingly bright. 'We'll go towards the rocks over there,' Col said, 'where the gulls are diving. That means there are fish. A school of mackerel, probably, chasing the sand-eels the seals like.'

He showed her how to cast a line, how to draw the 'fly' through the water to tempt the fish. The water was so clear she could see their silver backs with the dark markings. Below them, the deep forest of weed waved gently. Overhead, seagulls wheeled and dived and squawked.

'Got one!' Col wound in the line.

Grace watched the silver fish twist and flap. 'Oh! Poor thing!'

Col unhooked it and hit it sharply against the side of the boat. 'It's over quick enough,' he said. 'They don't suffer.' Col was matter of fact. 'It's what you have to do, if you want to eat. It's the nature of things: life, and death.'

Grace swallowed hard. She didn't watch the next time he caught a fish. But she thought about what he'd said. She understood what he meant. It wasn't any worse than eating fish and chips, or buying meat in a supermarket. If anything, it was more honest. You ate what you caught. The fish had a good, free life until the end.

'Your turn,' Col said. 'Imagine we're on a deserted island and it's all we have to eat. If we don't catch fish we'll die.'

Grace tried. She cast the line and waited for a fish to take the bait. 'You'll have to do the killing part,' she said, 'if I do catch one.' But her heart wasn't in it. She handed the rod back to Col without catching anything. She was happier watching for seals.

Two seals, now, were swimming near the boat. She could see the shadowy shape of their sleek bodies under the water. They stopped and dangled in the water, just their heads bobbing above.

'I've never been so close to wild seals before,' she whispered. 'It's amazing.'

'They're all around the island. They haul up on the rocks to sunbathe on sunny days. I'll show you, if you want.' Col looked at Grace. 'Dad gets cross because they take the fish and mess with the nets. But they're a protected species so we can't do anything about them.'

'Like hunt them, you mean?' Grace was shocked. She'd seen horrible pictures on television once, of people killing baby seals. It made her feel sick, that someone could do that.

Col shrugged. 'We're not allowed to harm them. We just get along beside them best we can. There's enough fish around here for us all, at the moment. Maybe not for ever.' He picked up the oars. 'We might as well row back and cook our mackerel. If we go now, there's time to make a fire on the beach. I have to help Dad, later.'

Grace was pleased she already knew how to make a fire. They rolled some big stones to make a circle to contain the fire, and piled up small bits of driftwood to make a lattice. The small pebbly beach was sheltered from the wind. Grace took off the life jacket and her jumper.

Col went to find matches and more dry driftwood in the boat shed. He brought back a rusty old grill, too, for cooking the fish on. The smaller bits of wood caught alight easily, cracking and spitting as the flames licked up the sticks. When it was all burning well Col added larger bits of driftwood, feeding them into the fire one at a time.

'When the flames go down and the wood goes white hot, that's the time to cook.' Col sliced the fish along their bellies and scooped out the livery innards. He chucked the red stuff into the sea and the gulls swooped down at once to eat it.

Grace watched. She wasn't sure she felt hungry any more.

She changed her mind when she smelt the sweet, smoky fish beginning to go toasty and crisp.

'Fish cooked over a wood fire on a beach is the tastiest thing in the whole world,' Col said. He turned the pieces of fish over with a stick, to grill the other side.

'I've never tried, before,' Grace said. Today was the first time for lots of things.

Col was right. The mackerel tasted amazing, even if it was hard to pick out all the tiny bones. She licked her fingers and then ran down to the sea to wash her hands properly. Col was already packing things up, kicking sand over the embers of the fire to put them out. 'Got to go and help Dad now,' he said. 'Shall we race the boats tomorrow?'

'Yes,' Grace said. 'I've made a sail for mine. I want to try it out.'

Grace walked up the lane to the beach road, back towards Granny's house. The wind had got up: it blew her hair back from her face and made goosebumps on her bare arms. She put her jumper back on. She wasn't ready to go back inside. She found a footpath through the dune grass onto the edge of the sandy beach that ran all along this side of the island.

The tide was still going down; it left ridges in the wet sand and sandy pools and treasures: she picked up a piece of green sea-glass, polished smooth by the waves, and then a blue piece, and three perfect white shells. They'd make a beautiful necklace, Grace thought, if she could find a way to thread them onto a string. She could make one for Molly, and one for Granny.

A seal was swimming parallel to the beach, as if it were keeping step with her. Every so often Grace stopped, and the seal stopped too. It raised its head to watch her. She waved to it. 'Hello, seal!' Was it the same one she'd seen before? Perhaps it was getting used to her. She could make friends with it. Even swim with it, maybe.

Granny was sitting outside on the deck, chatting to a man with curly grey hair and a smiley face. Grace recognised him from somewhere. Oh yes, the Giddy Goat café.

'Was it fun?' Granny called down to her. 'Did you catch a fish?'

'I didn't, but Col caught five and we ate one each. We cooked them on the beach. Col's mum will have the rest.'

'You won't need dinner today, then,' Granny said. She laughed at the sad face Grace made. 'I'm teasing you,' she said. 'I know very well that being out on a boat makes you extra hungry.'

Grace held out the pieces of glass for Granny to see. 'I'm collecting more treasure,' she called up.

'Show me later,' Granny said. 'I can't see very well from here without my glasses.'

Granny's friend waved at Grace as she ran on again, searching the tide line. There were more people on the beach today. Small children clambered over the rocks, fishing with nets in the pools. Grace felt cross. This was her beach. Hers and Granny's and Col's. And then she felt bad, because of course it wasn't really. You couldn't own a beach. But there had been something very special about being the only person on it, before.

She stopped running to see what the children were all looking at, pointing. They'd seen her seal, she realized. She—Grace was sure it was a she—was there again, holding her whiskery head out of the water. The rest of her body dangled underwater, a vertical, shadowy shape below. The seal was watching the children, now, as they ran to the end of the rocky outcrop and shouted. Two of them threw pebbles at the seal and it dived under.

Grace felt hot with anger. Why would you throw stones at an animal, as if you wanted to scare or hurt it? She turned away.

At bedtime, Grace asked Granny to finish telling her the story about the fisherman and the Selkie.

'Where did we get to before?' Granny asked. 'I'm not quite sure at which point you fell asleep.'

'He'd hidden her seal-skin. So she couldn't go back to the sea.'

'Yes. Well, the fisherman loved his beautiful wife, with her long, dark hair and her big brown eyes. She loved him back, and they were happy enough for many years and had five beautiful children together: all boys. But even though she loved her sons and laughed and sang and played with them, most evenings when her work was done, the woman would go down to the beach. She would watch the sun setting over the sea and her heart was full of longing and sadness, for without her seal-skin she could never go back under the water again.

'One day, her youngest son went with her, and asked her why she was sad. She told him her story, about who she really was: a Selkie, half seal, half woman. She told him about her skin, which had been taken away from her when she was a young woman.

'Her son, who loved his mother very much, remembered something his father had shown him a long time ago, hidden in a space between the stones in the big kitchen fireplace. He ran back to the house and found the mottled grey skin in the hiding place, now tattered and dull, not gleaming and beautiful as it had once been, and he took it to his mother where she still sat on the beach staring out to sea. She was filled with joy, and she kissed her boy, took the skin and put it on, and slipped into the waves. She turned once, to say farewell to her dear child, and then she dived beneath the surface and was gone.'

Grace turned to look at Granny. Were those tears on her face?

'Did she come back to see her family?' Grace asked.

'The story doesn't say. I think she was gone for ever, back to her Selkie folk. But I expect from time to time she swam back to the bay, and looked at the white cottage and checked that her land family were safe and well. Her sons were all grown up by then, and they didn't need her anymore.'

'But that's sad,' Grace said. And what about the fisherman? Wasn't he lonely again?'

'Well, he shouldn't really have hidden her skin, should he? He should have known about her true nature, that she needed the sea as well as the land.'

Grace still thought it was too sad.

'Well, some stories do have sad endings. It couldn't have a happy ending for them both, because they needed different things.'

Grace thought about that. 'And the fisherman had all his sons, and soon he'd have grandchildren to make him happy and keep him company.'

'Yes,' Granny said. 'Having grandchildren made him very happy indeed.' She kissed the top of Grace's head. 'Time for sleep, darling girl.'

Grace lay in the dark bedroom listening to the shooshing sound of the sea. Somewhere out there, her seal was swimming, happy and free.

Chapter 6

Otters

Grace and Granny were eating porridge at the kitchen table. It was too cold to have breakfast outside this morning: the wind was blowing hard from the west, Granny said. The weather was changing again. A storm was forecast.

'That's exciting!' Grace said. She hadn't seen a proper big storm before, but Grandpa used to talk about them. Rare birds got blown in on the gales. All sorts of flotsam and jetsam would wash up on the beach.

'There's Col.' Granny pointed through the window.

Col was running along the sand, a wooden boat with a brown sail held high in one hand. He was playing a game as usual: he looked as if he was sailing the boat through the air, tackling stormy seas and possibly a pirate attack.

Grace laughed. 'He doesn't know we're watching,' she said. She waved at him when he got close enough to see, and opened the door to let him in.

Col ran up the wooden steps to the deck. 'Boat race?' he asked Grace. His cheeks were pink from the wind.

'We're still having breakfast,' Grace said. 'Can you wait a minute?'

Col chatted while Grace ate her porridge. He told them about seeing otters, over the other side of the island. There were at least five: two adults and three cubs. While he talked, Col wandered around the house, picking things up and looking at them. He was curious about everything. Granny didn't seem to mind.

'It's very tidy,' Col said. He grinned. 'Not like ours.'

'It's easy to be tidy when you live by yourself like me,' Granny said. 'But your mum and dad have got their hands full, looking after the family and working so hard. Is your little brother sleeping better now?'

'No,' Col said. 'He doesn't like sleeping in a bed! But the baby needs the cot: he's too big for the Moses basket.'

Grace ran to get her driftwood boat from her bedroom. She shoved her feet into boots and put on her jacket. 'We're going to the rock pools in Seal Bay to sail our boats. Is that all right?'

Granny nodded. 'Keep an eye on the tide. And be back for lunch. You can have some too, Col, if you'd like that. I'll bake potatoes in the oven.'

Grace and Col ran together along the sandy beach as far as the rocks, and then climbed back up to the road to go past the headland and down onto the next bay. The wind was blowing hard, rippling the dune grass. It made the small white sail on her boat flap and quiver too, as if it was trying to escape.

Down on the beach, it was more sheltered. This bay was a huge crescent of white sand, bigger even than Granny's beach. A platform of rock stretched all along this side, dotted with small rock pools and covered with seaweed. Closer to the water, the pools were huge: perfect for sailing the boats. Col ran over the slippery rocks, hardly missing a beat.

Grace went more slowly, picking her way, looking

into the mysterious worlds contained in each rock pool. They were teeming with life: tiny green crabs, and speckled fish, shrimps and anemones. She spotted a bright orange starfish and hunkered down to watch the way it moved its arms as it crossed the sandy bottom of a pool.

'Hurry up!' Col shouted and she jumped up again and walked down the rocks to join him.

Brrr. It was colder, closer to the sea. The waves crashed and boomed. Col and Grace lowered their boats onto a large, wide rock-pool and watched as the wind filled the sails and took each boat immediately, whisking them across the water. A great gust of wind toppled Grace's boat for a second. Would it be swamped and sink? But no, the little boat wobbled and steadied and came upright again, changing tack and catching up with Col's.

'A tie,' Col said, generously, as they ran round to pick up the boats the other side.

Grace laughed. 'No, yours won. But we can race again. Best of three?'

A lull in the wind: the boats struggled to move at all. They were too far out for them to reach. Col went searching for a stick, but before he came back the wind had picked up and blown the boats on and this time Grace's boat won.

And the next.

Col didn't care. 'Got to go back anyway,' he said. 'Supposed to be helping my nan in the shop. The ferry delivery comes this morning. Race you.' He was already running, slipping on the shiny wet weed, back up to the road.

Grace chased after him. She was good at running; she caught him up easily and overtook.

'Can you do cartwheels?' she asked him. She did one, to show him, and he tried, and was rubbish. He tried again. 'Better. You just need to practise,' Grace said.

'Want to see those otters?' Col asked. They were almost back at the house.

'Yes,' Grace said. 'Where, exactly?'

'Other side of the island. You'll need a bike. Have you got one?'

Grace shook her head. 'Only Granny's, and it's too big for me.'

'You can hire them at the garage in the village,' Col said. 'Anyhow, I've got to go. See you later!'

Grace watched him. He ran along for a bit, then stopped to do a cartwheel. He collapsed in a heap, got up, ran on again, stopped to try another cartwheel. Grace smiled. He was nice, Col. Already he felt like a proper friend.

Granny came out of the kitchen onto the deck. She waved at Grace. 'Where's Col going? Isn't he staying for lunch?' she called down.

'No. He's got to help in the shop or something.' Grace climbed up the wooden steps and flopped down on one of the chairs. 'I need a bike. Can we hire me one, Granny? Please?' She explained about the otters.

'Well,' Granny said, 'it sounds like a good idea. It would be easier for you to get around the island, for sure. And it would be fun for you. I'll ask around.'

'They have bikes you can hire at the garage, Col said.'

'All right. We'll go and see, later. At least there isn't much traffic to worry about on the island. Do you think your mum and dad would be happy about it?' Granny asked. 'I'll phone them to check.'

After lunch—her favourite baked potatoes and baked beans with grated cheese—Grace listened while Granny chatted to Mum. Then it was her turn.

'What have you been doing?' Mum asked.

Grace told her about her driftwood boat and going fishing with Col. She told her about making necklaces from beach treasure. 'And please tell Granny I can ride a bike because that means I can go with Col to see some otters on the other side of the island.'

'Lucky you,' Mum said. 'I've never seen otters in the wild. But you must be very, very careful riding on the roads, Grace.' The worry sound was in Mum's voice.

For a moment, Grace held her breath, wondering if Mum was going to change her mind and say Grace couldn't ride the bike after all.

But Mum carried on talking about home. 'It's very strange without you. Kit's been a bit bored and naughty, and I think the babies are teething . . .'

It was hard to imagine family life going on without her. Grace thought about Kit and the babies and for a moment she missed them all so much it hurt.

Mum was still talking. 'So Kit's gone next door to play with Marek while I get on with the washing and later I'll do a big supermarket shop. The twins are having their nap. Dad's at work.'

Grace thought about her bedroom at home. The pictures and photos pinned up on the board. Her old soft toys, arranged neatly on the shelf above the bed now she was too old to play with them. The furry white seal had been a present from Granny and Grandpa when she was a baby . . .

'Send us a postcard!' Mum said. 'Tell us all about the otters. Kit would like that. Now, I'll say goodbye to you, darling, and just have a last word with Granny.'

'Bye Mum. Love you!' Grace said. She handed the phone back to Granny. She wandered back out to the deck and looked out over the beach. The sky was grey: big clouds were building up out at sea. No sign of her seal now.

The garage was at the other end of the village beyond the shop. It was a big shed, really, with one petrol pump and one diesel pump outside, and a load of rusty-looking cars waiting to be mended. The bikes for hire were chained to a stand at the back of the shed. Granny and Grace went with the man to have a look.

'Try this one for size,' the man said, unlocking a blue and silver bike with big tyres.

'It's a lovely colour!' Granny said. 'Very smart.'

Grace practised going up and down the road near the Garage. She hadn't forgotten how to balance, even though it was ages since she'd ridden a bike. She'd long outgrown hers, and it belonged to Kit now, for mucking about in the park.

'Looks about right,' the man said. 'How does it feel? Want the saddle raised a bit?'

'No thanks,' Grace said. She felt more secure when she could put both feet down easily. She tried the bike bell and made it ring out.

'I'll do you a special price,' the man told Granny. 'Islanders' rate, and I'll throw in two panniers as part of the deal.'

Panniers turned out to mean two bags that clipped on a rack at the back, for carrying things. 'You can put a picnic in there,' Granny said. 'And a towel and swimming things.'

'Not today. No way! It's not warm enough for swimming.' From here Grace could see the grey sea, the tops of the waves flicked into white crests by the wind.

Grace rode the bike back to Granny's house, and Granny walked behind. For the rest of the afternoon, Grace practised riding up and down the road and

doing the gears. When she was tired of that, she went inside to make her beach treasure into jewellery. She was still busy when Col turned up again, this time riding his own old bike.

He came straight in and stood in the doorway, watching. 'What are you doing?'

Grace showed him the necklace she was threading. 'I found every bit of it on the beach,' she said. 'I had to search for small shells and sea-glass which already had holes in. It was too difficult to make holes myself; the shells kept breaking. Even the blue string comes from the beach.'

'Oh.' Col didn't seem very interested. 'Shall we go, then? Did you get a bike?'

'Yes!' Grace pointed to it, leant against the wall of the house. They went outside together for a better look.

'Smart!' Col said. 'Can I try it out?' He rode it up the road and back to the house while Grace watched. 'It's better than mine,' he told her. 'It's a proper mountain bike for off-road.'

Granny came out to wave them off. 'Be very careful,' she said. 'There aren't many cars, but there are always a few. Tractors too. Just get off the road if you hear one coming, well out of the way.'

'I'll be fine, Granny!' Grace hugged her. 'Don't worry about me.'

It was exciting, riding along the single-track road. It seemed so fast compared to the walk to the Giddy Goat café she'd done the other day with Granny. She and Col went the same direction to begin with, passing the café on the way over to the opposite side of the island.

The road was mostly flat: she could see for miles over fields of barley and inland pools reflecting sky. At one point, from the top of a slight hill, she could see sea in every direction. 'It makes you realize how small the island is, really,' Grace said.

Col shrugged. 'It's big enough,' he said. 'It's got everything you need.' He sounded a bit cross.

Grace wondered if he thought she was criticizing the island, or something. 'It's the perfect size. It's totally lovely,' she told him.

Everywhere there were birds: geese and wild ducks and swans on the inland water, and flocks of small brown birds taking off from the fields as they cycled past. The landscape changed, from farmed fields divided by stone walls to rough open ground covered by heather and gorse. A stream ran between peaty banks, the water a deep gold.

'Are we nearly there?' Grace asked. Her legs were beginning to ache.

'Very nearly,' Col said. 'And it's mostly downhill. We have to leave the bikes behind and walk the last few metres. And keep very quiet, so we don't scare the otters if they are about.'

Grace followed Col, treading in his footsteps along the edge of the small stream as it flowed towards the sea onto a pebbly, seaweedy bit of beach.

Col stopped to show her a patch of brighter green grass. 'It's like that because it's fertilized by otter poo,' he whispered. 'The poo's called *spraint*. They do it in the same places each time, to leave their scent. Marking out their patch.' A bit further on, he showed her the faint path through the rough grass and heather, and a paw print in the soft earth.

Col suddenly stopped still. 'Sshh!' he said, even though Grace wasn't making any noise. She stopped too. Col beckoned her, and she crept forward quietly till she was next to him, close to an old stone wall.

'There!' he whispered. 'We're in luck. It's coming this way, up from the beach.'

Grace saw movement through the low heather; something definitely was there. It stopped still. She saw the brown head, the wet fur slicked back, and brown eyes. Her heart beat fast. It was exciting, to see such a rare animal in the wild, busy with its own life. But the otter was sniffing the air, alert to danger, and it turned and ran back towards the beach. She heard the *plop* as it dived into the water and swam away to safety.

Col grinned. 'Magic, eh? Pity it got scared so quick.'

'I hardly saw it,' Grace said. 'If you hadn't been here, I'd have missed it completely.'

'They spend lots of time in the sea, searching for crabs and fish among the rocks and in the kelp,' Col explained. 'But they have to come back inland to rinse their fur in fresh water. The lochans are perfect for that. Lochans are like ponds,' he explained.

'So, shall we wait for it to come back?'

'We can wait for a while if you like. But now it knows we're here, it'll most likely stay hidden.'

Grace found a dryish clump of heather to sit on and settled down. Col did the same. He was good at being totally still, Grace thought. The only sounds were the call of birds and the wind in the dry grass. In his faded jeans and green jumper he blended in with the landscape so you'd hardly know he was there.

Grace shifted position. Her legs ached. She yawned.

Col stood up. 'Let's go. We can come back another time.'

'What shall we do now?' Grace asked. She turned the collar of her coat up: it was colder than ever in the wind.

'Come back to mine if you want,' Col said. 'Mum said to ask you.'

'OK, if you're sure she won't mind,' Grace said. She was remembering the untidy house, and Kate's tired face. Suddenly she felt nervous.

Chapter 7

Col's House

Col led Grace round the back of the terrace of houses. A grassy footpath went along the backs of the houses. He opened a green gate, into a small yard full of bits and pieces of boat stuff and broken flowerpots and old rusty ride-on toys. They went in through the back door.

Col's mum, Kate, was stirring something at the stove. She smiled at them. 'Hello again, Grace!'

'Hello,' Grace said.

Col's little brother was sitting at the table, scribbling in chunky felt-tip pens on an old envelope. He waved a pen in the air. 'Col! Cat!'

Col leant over his brother, and drew a silly picture of a cat with big whiskers and a round blob of body and a sticky-out tail. 'You draw him one,' Col said and he handed Grace the pen.

Grace flushed. She didn't mean to show off, but her drawing was a million times better than Col's. It actually looked like a real cat.

Col's mum, Kate, peered over to see. 'Wow! That's brilliant, Grace. Isn't it lovely, Benny?'

Benny didn't say anything. He was colouring in the cat, going over the lines and spoiling it. Grace didn't mind. It was the sort of thing Kit used to do when he was three.

Kate put the biscuit tin on the table and poured mugs of tea for Grace and Col. Grace didn't like to say she hated the taste of tea. It sounded rude. Upstairs, the baby started to wail. Kate sighed. She went out of the kitchen.

'Do you want mine?' Grace pushed her mug towards Col. 'I don't drink tea.'

'Why didn't you say?'

'I didn't want to be rude to your mum.'

'She wouldn't mind about a thing like that! It's better to say what you think straight out. Not pretend.' He took Grace's mug of tea and poured it down the sink. 'There. Sorted!'

Benny pushed his paper towards Grace. 'More cat?' he asked. Grace drew him a whole family of cats, with kittens and aunty and uncle and cousin cats. 'Do them different colours,' she said. She showed him what she meant. 'This one can be tabby, and that one's marmalade with white paws, and the daddy one could be black and white . . . '

Benny picked up the orange felt-tip and scribbled over all the cats.

'Nice try,' Col said.

Kate came back in, the baby over her shoulder. She sat down at the table, hitched up her top, and settled the baby for a breastfeed. Grace looked away, embarrassed. Kate chatted away the whole time. She asked Grace lots of questions about her family. She started asking about Granny and Grandpa. Grace felt her face go hot.

'Come and see my room?' Col asked Grace. He seemed to understand that it was hard for her to talk about her grandpa. 'I'll show you my collection.'

Grace followed him upstairs. Col's tiny bedroom was at the front of the house, overlooking the harbour.

She stood at the window. The tide was high; one of the fishing trawlers was just going out to sea through the gap in the harbour wall. 'Is that your dad's boat?' Grace asked.

Col shook his head. 'Dad's boat went this morning, on the high tide. He won't be back till dark. Unless the weather gets worse before then: they'll probably head back if it looks like the storm's coming.'

'Do you ever go out in the boat with him?'

'Mum doesn't like me going. It's dangerous, with all the machinery and the slippery deck and all that.'

'Will you be a fisherman when you grow up?'

'Yes. If there's any lobsters left by then.'

'And will you stay living here?'

'Yes, of course. Why would I want to go anywhere else?'

'Because there are so many places in the world! So much to discover.' Grace couldn't imagine what it would be like to stay in one place your whole life, even a place as amazing as this. But Col was different from her. And he knew so much about the island: the birds and the animals and about how to survive. That was pretty special, wasn't it? Maybe that was more important than simply visiting lots of different places.

She turned away from the window. There wasn't much space in the bedroom, what with two beds and an old wooden table with an ancient computer on the top. She sat down on one of the beds.

Col's collection, lined up along a shelf above his bed, was made up of tiny bird skulls, scoured clean by the sea and dried by the sun and the wind, sea urchin shells, and some funny brown seeds like beans, which

Col said had been washed over from land the other side of the Atlantic Ocean.

Grace picked up one of the skulls. 'It's so light!' she said. 'Tiny. Birds must have tiny brains!'

'That one's a tern skull,' Col told her. 'Know what a tern looks like?'

Grace shook her head.

Col turned on the computer and it whirred slowly into action. He pulled a face. 'Internet's rubbish here.' Eventually, the page came up. Grace looked at the picture of an arctic tern: a small, grey bird shaped like a swallow, with a black head and red beak and legs.

'It might be tiny, but it can navigate all the way from the Antarctic to here, by the stars and the earth's magnetic forces. They migrate further than any other bird.'

'You know a lot,' Grace said.

Col shrugged. 'I know about island things, birds and otters and that.'

'And seals.'

'Yes, seals too.'

Grace looked round the walls in Col's room. The paint was peeling and there was a mouldy patch of damp in one corner near the window. She shivered.

'You don't have any pictures up in here,' she said.

'Why would I need pictures?'

'Because they are nice. I mean, they brighten things up and make you happy. It's not about *needing* them, exactly.'

'I can look at things on the computer,' Col said. 'Or outside, for real, which is a million times better.' He put the skull back in its place on the shelf. 'I'll show you a real arctic tern, if you want. And the place the seals go to bask.'

There were no books in Col's room, either, Grace noticed, but she didn't say anything. Raised voices were coming from downstairs.

'Col?' Kate called up. 'I need you to come down, right now!'

'I'd better go,' Grace said. It made her uncomfortable, hearing Kate telling Benny off. Benny was beginning to cry. Her own mum hardly ever lost her temper with Kit or the babies, even when she was tired and too busy. She was cross with Dad sometimes, but not very often, and rarely with Grace.

She clattered down the bare wooden staircase after Col.

'Bye, Benny. Thanks-for-having-me-Kate,' she said really quickly, so the words all ran together. She ran out of the back door to get her bike. She could hear Kate telling Col he had to go and get the shopping from his nan at the post office shop. Grace walked along the lane, pushing the bike, half hoping that Col would catch her up and they could go along the road together. But he didn't appear, and she walked on by herself.

She'd not been concentrating. She'd gone the wrong way along the lane; she only realized when she found herself passing the boat shed. She kept going anyway, following the lane as it looped back to the village. It came out near the church. Grace pushed the bike across the grass, to cut the corner.

There was Grandpa's grave, right in front of her. It came as a shock, to come across his name, *Robert Woodruff*, carved on the stone, simply because she'd not been thinking about it. She laid the bike down on the grass, and knelt down to tidy up the flowers. Some of them had died: she took them out but that meant the ones left behind looked a bit lonely, so she went to see if there were any wild flowers growing in the longer grass near the bank. She found a patch of pink flowers, and some sprigs of heather, and took them back to put in the jam jar. 'There you are, Grandpa,' she said out loud.

Beloved husband, father and grandfather, it said on the stone beneath his name and the dates of his life. It was almost exactly one year since he died. Grace shivered. She didn't want to think about Grandpa like this. She wanted to remember him when he was alive, whittling a piece of driftwood to make a boat, or playing cricket with her and Kit on the beach, or singing along to the radio. His arms cuddling her in a bear hug and the smell of his jumper and his stubbly face that tickled . . .

Her eyes prickled with tears. She picked the bike up and wheeled it out of the churchyard and onto the road. There was no sign of Col; no sign of anyone in the village—except three silly sheep, who ran in front of the bike, bleating. The sign at the garage blew back and forth, the metal chain squeaking.

It was hard work, cycling along the beach road against the wind. It stung her eyes and made her nose run. The wind was full of tiny bits of sand, whipped up from the beach. Out at sea, the waves were all topped with white. The sky hung heavy with cloud; the first rain was beginning to spit as Grace finally reached Granny's house.

Granny was sitting in the window seat, watching the sea through binoculars. 'The storm's blowing in,' she told Grace. 'I'm glad you're safely home.' She put the binoculars back down and looked at Grace. 'Are you all right, darling? You were such a long time!'

'I went back to Col's house,' Grace explained. 'We did see an otter, but it ran away again.'

Granny stretched out her back and stood up. 'Come and tell me all about it while I make myself a cup of tea.'

'Why do grown-ups drink tea all the time?' Grace asked her.

Granny laughed. 'It's a comfort, that's what. You'll be the same when you're my age!'

'No way!' Grace said.

'How were things at Col's house?' Granny asked.

'OK. His mum was a bit stressy. And his computer is ever so old.'

'Things are difficult for Col's family at the moment,' Granny said. 'Fishing doesn't bring in much of a wage these days and Kate can't work with a baby and a toddler to look after. But Col's a good lad. He does his share. More than.'

'It was cold and damp in Col's room,' Grace told her. 'It isn't very cosy there.'

The wind was getting stronger. Through the kitchen window, Grace watched the waves rolling in up the beach, the surf whipped into white froth. Was that someone swimming in the rough water? Surely not. She screwed up her eyes to see better. Three dark heads. She ran to get the binoculars from the window seat in the living room.

Everything looked fuzzy and weird. Grace turned the bit in the middle of the binoculars to bring everything into focus again. Now she could see clearly: the three dark heads were seals, not people. And there were more: four, five, six, seven seals, Grace counted. She watched them riding the breakers into the bay. 'The seals are surfing like people!' Grace told Granny. 'Just for the fun of it.'

'Perhaps they are Selkies, not seals at all,' Granny said. 'If you keep watching, you'll see them come up the beach and peel off their seal-skins and be people again!'

'Don't be silly, Granny.'

Granny shrugged. She sipped her tea and didn't say anything else.

Grace stared out of the window. The seals had disappeared again. She felt lonely, suddenly. The house seemed empty with no one to play with or talk to except Granny today. Col was busy. It was too cold to go down to the beach, and there was nothing to do here. No computer or games apart from old-fashioned board ones. She wandered back to the living room and looked through Granny's stack of DVDs but there was nothing she hadn't seen already.

'Put some music on,' Granny called out. 'Something cheerful.'

Grace found a CD of some fiddle music she knew Granny liked. She heard Granny dancing round the kitchen as the tune picked up pace. She curled up on the cushions on the window seat and leafed through Granny's book about island wildlife. She flicked to the page about otters, and then she looked up terns and scallops. She found the names of the pink flowers she'd picked earlier: *ragged robin*.

'I'm making fish pie for tea,' Granny called out. 'Your favourite. And afterwards, I'll get the sewing machine out and finish making your new skirt.'

Grace cheered up a bit. After tea, while Granny sewed, she could do her painting of the day: a picture for Col, perhaps, to stick on his wall. An otter or a seal or an arctic tern? Otter, she decided.

Grace was excited about the new skirt Granny was making her. It was the colour of the sea: bluey-green, woven through with a thread of gold that sparkled in the light. Granny had bought the material a long time ago, when she was on holiday in India; she had forgotten all about it. And then, when they were looking for the scrap of cotton to make a sail for the boat, Granny had found the material neatly folded in a paper bag. 'It's pure silk,' Granny had said, holding out the length of material. 'And it matches your eyes perfectly.'

At bedtime, Granny came in to say goodnight. She pulled the curtains tight. Rain was bashing against the window glass, the wind howling like a wild cat trying to get inside. 'It's a wild stormy night,' Granny said. 'Let's hope all the fishing boats are safely back in the harbour.'

Grace remembered what Col had said about slippery decks and dangerous machinery. She tried to imagine what it would be like out at sea in the darkness and the storm.

'I'll read you a poem instead of a story tonight,' Granny said. She took a book with a red cover from one of the bookshelves. She blew the sand off the pages and laughed. 'Sand gets everywhere, even in here!' She leafed through the pages. 'Grandpa loved this one. It's called "Windy Nights".' She began to read:

'Whenever the moon and stars are set
Whenever the wind is high
All night long in the dark and wet,
A man goes riding by.'

Grace listened intently as Granny read out the poem. Granny read well, so that the words made pictures and sounds in Grace's head.

'Why does he gallop about? The man in the poem?' Grace asked.

'I don't know. What do you think?'

'I reckon he's not a real man, but a ghost man, on a ghost horse. That's why he rides at night when it's stormy. He died on a journey in a storm and now he's forever riding and riding . . .'

Outside, the storm lashed the window. The rhythm of the drumming rain was a bit like horses' hooves, Grace thought. She and Granny were quiet, listening as the wind picked up even more.

'If you listen hard enough,' Granny said, 'you can hear all sorts in the wind.'

'Like what?' Grace burrowed deeper under the duvet so her shoulders were covered.

'When I'm here alone, sometimes I hear voices on the wind. I've opened the door more than once, thinking someone's calling out to me.' Granny shivered. 'But, of course, there's never anyone there. It's me, imagining things.' Granny noticed Grace's face. 'I didn't mean to make you afraid, darling.'

'I'm not really frightened,' she said. 'I like it that you imagine things. I do that, too.'

'I expect that's where most old stories come from,'

Granny said. 'People sitting round a fire on a stormy night, letting their imaginations run riot, each person trying to tell a better story than the one before, getting wilder and more creative each time.' She was quiet for a moment. 'And maybe we hear what we *want* to hear in the wind.' She had that faraway look on her face that Grace had seen before, when Granny thought about Grandpa.

Grace reached out to touch Granny's hand.

Granny squeezed her hand back. 'Right, now it's time for sleep. The nice thing about the wind is that it makes you think how good it is to be warm and dry and safe inside. By daybreak, the storm will have passed over and it will be a clear bright morning with all sorts of new treasures washed up on the beach. Sleep well, Grace darling!'

Grace and Granny both laughed. It was Granny's old joke: there had been an actual, real girl called Grace Darling once upon a time, the daughter of a lighthouse keeper.

Grace lay in the dark, remembering the story Granny had told her about Grace Darling bravely rowing a tiny boat out in a storm to help her father rescue people from a wrecked ship on the rocks near the Farne Islands. The rescue made Grace Darling famous, but she didn't like being famous. And then she got ill and she died so it was a sad story too . . .

Grace didn't want to think about sad things. She thought instead about new treasures washing up on the beach, and going out to look first thing in the morning, and she gradually got sleepier and she must soon have fallen asleep.

She woke up in the dead of night. Only this night was very much alive. The wind was still rattling the windows, howling down the chimney, screeching and shaking the whole house as if it was angry and wanted to break the house into tiny pieces. The sounds changed. Now the wind moaned and whined. It cried like a lost child. Grace had to put her fingers in her ears and even that wasn't enough to keep out the pitiful sound.

Words from Granny's poem jiggled in her head and mixed with her half-dreaming thoughts and the sounds of the storm . . . *when ships are tossed at sea* . . . Imagine being on a boat in this . . . Grace Darling rowing out to save people from the wrecked ship . . . floundering in the icy water . . .

At last the rain got less heavy and the wind dropped enough for her to fall back to sleep.

Chapter 8

After the Storm

It wasn't the clear sunny morning Granny had promised. It was still raining, and the wind rattled the roof slates, whistled down the chimney: howled and shrieked and wrapped the house round with its moaning sounds.

'Can I go out, to watch the big waves?' Grace asked.

'It's too wet,' Granny said. 'And it's not safe anywhere near that sea with those huge waves breaking. You have to respect the sea when it's as wild as this.'

After breakfast, Granny settled herself in the conservatory and turned on the radio to listen to the local news. Grace wandered into the living room and curled up on the window seat, nose pressed to the glass to watch the waves crashing and roaring up the beach. The windows were coated with a fine film of sea-spray: that's what the word *spindrift* meant, the name of Granny's house.

There was no sign of seals today; or if they were out there, Grace couldn't see them, even with the binoculars. She gave up looking after a while. She knelt down in front of Granny's bookshelves, hunting for something good to read. She liked the title *Tarka the Otter*. The book had lovely drawings, too. She tried to read the first chapter but the sentences were a bit old-fashioned and difficult. She put the book back, and took out a story called *Seal Morning* instead. The girl in the story was ten, and she kept all sorts of wild animals, like otters, rats, squirrels, and deer, and most wonderful of all, a seal called Lora. But that book, too, had long sentences and difficult words like *conveniences* and *entailed* and *crepitation* that muddled her head. Grace skipped over the boring bits she didn't understand.

Grace put the book down on the window seat. The rain had stopped: she could see a break in the cloud, a patch of grey-blue sky. The wind was softer too, and now the tide was lower the waves weren't so big and frightening. From the conservatory, the sound of the radio droned on.

Grace got her coat from the hook in the hall, and slipped her bare feet into boots. 'The rain's stopped and I'm going down to the beach to look for treasures, Granny!' she called. 'The tide's low enough, now.'

'OK,' Granny called back. 'Take care, and be back for lunch.'

Grace opened the back door and took a gulp of fresh air. It smelt different, after the storm, as if the air itself had been washed clean. But there were other new smells too, as she went down the steps and got closer to the beach. Fishy and salty and strange. The sea had come right up the beach in the storm: the sand at the top was littered with flotsam and jetsam.

There were wooden planks from a broken-up boat; masses of stinky seaweed already swarming with eager flies; plastic bottles of all colours and pieces of rope, old shoes, a big metal barrel, and a load of broken plastic crates. Grace wrinkled up her nose at the smell as the rubbish gently steamed in the early morning sun. A huge white and grey gull flew up as Grace came close, and settled itself a little further on, picking over the debris with its big yellow beak.

Grace ran along, searching for treasure. She kicked a pile of brown weed and found two heart-shaped sea beans, a bit like the ones in Col's collection. There were small green crabs hidden among the weed, and she crouched down to look at one more closely. On a patch of fine silver white sand further along the beach she came across a heap of tiny pink-striped cowrie shells. She stuffed her pockets with the shells. They would be perfect for making a necklace. She spotted a big white shell and when she went closer she realized it was a bird skull, bleached by the sea and scoured clean by the sand. She picked it up very carefully and wrapped it in a tissue in her pocket. She would give it to Col for his collection.

Now she was at the end of the beach, the temptation to go on round to the next bay was too strong to resist. She stood up straight for a moment and looked back to check whether Granny was watching her from the house, but it was much too far away to tell. In any case, Granny was relaxed about Grace doing things by herself now: she'd let her go out in the boat with Col, and ride the bike over the island, hadn't she? So she wouldn't mind.

Grace half hoped she'd see Col running along the beach to join her, but the expanse of sand was deserted except for the seabirds which were everywhere this early morning, picking over the fresh debris from the storm.

Grace climbed up the rocks, went along the road to the next bay and down again to the big outcrop of rocks where she'd come before with Col. The high tide had left the pools brimming with clear water that reflected the sunlight beginning to come through the cloud. It was so dazzlingly bright that for a second she could see nothing at all.

She listened. There was a sound coming from further down the rocks. Not a bird, more like a cross between a puppy's yelp and the *maa* of a lamb. Something moved out of the shadow at the edge of a boulder, and the shape took form and she realized what she was looking at.

A baby seal.

It was small, with speckled pale skin, and it was staring sorrowfully at her with huge dark eyes, crying. It tried to move its front flippers, and rocked and shuffled, trying to move away from her down the rocks and failing miserably.

Grace stared.

The baby seal flopped and floundered in a panic to get away, but it couldn't. It cried like a human baby.

Perhaps it had only just been born. Was the mother seal waiting nearby, scared because Grace was so close? Grace squeezed up her eyes against the sun, and scanned the sea and the rocks for signs of a mother seal.

The baby seal had stopped moving. It had given up. Perhaps it was going to die.

What could she do?

Col would know. But Col wasn't here.

Grace's heart raced. She looked back at the baby seal, now still and quiet in the shadow of the rock. It must be hungry as well as afraid. Perhaps it had been washed off its rock in the night by the storm and separated from its mother. The tide had left it stranded here. The pup was too weak to swim back. Too frightened and alone.

She tried to remember what the wildlife book said about seal pups. Harbour seal pups could swim within a day of being born; Col had told her that too. They slept on the rocks off shore, close to their mothers. They suckled rich seal milk from their mothers. Seal milk was much more oily and rich than cows' milk.

After three or four weeks, the pups were weaned and ate fish . . .

Perhaps she should wait—to see if the mother seal came searching for her pup. But how would the seal mother know where to look? There were miles of beaches, lots of different rocks and islands where it might have been swept by the storm. The chances of her finding the pup were almost none. This pup was less than a metre long; it wasn't old enough to eat fish, she was pretty sure.

Perhaps she should go and get some milk for the pup? Like in the *Seal Morning* book, where the girl had fed Lora with a baby's bottle of milk mixed with oil . . . That way, the seal pup would build its strength, and then it might be able to swim and find its own way back. Maybe seal pups, especially very young ones, had natural instincts about getting back to their mothers.

Grace spoke to the pup, keeping her voice steady and calm, so as not to frighten it even more. 'Don't cry, little one. I'm going to help you. I'll get you some milk. I won't be long.'

She wished she could go right up and stroke its soft head and comfort it. But the pup looked terrified of her. Maybe, if she brought it a bottle and it smelt the warm milk, it would let her get close?

'I'm coming back. Don't give up!'

The pup cried again, a sad little *maaa*.

Grace clambered back up the rocks, took one last look at the seal pup, and raced along the road. She ran the whole way to Granny's house, up the steps and burst into the kitchen to tell Granny what she'd found.

But Granny wasn't there. She wasn't in the conservatory, either. She wasn't in the bedroom or the bathroom. She must have gone out; perhaps she'd taken cakes to the Giddy Goat café or gone to see her friend Angus, or Flora at the post office. It was odd that she hadn't left a note for Grace, like she usually did.

Grace went back into the kitchen. She searched through the cupboards for one of the baby bottles Granny kept for the twins. She took milk from the fridge and warmed some in a pan on the stove. She added a drop of cooking oil: how much? She added a second drop, for luck. Carefully, she poured the milk into the baby bottle, screwed on the top with the teat, put on the blue plastic cap and shook the bottle to blend the oil with the milk.

Grace took a towel from the kitchen drawer and wrapped the bottle in it to keep it warm. She shoved it into one of the bike panniers, clipped the bag onto the bike. That would be quicker than running along the beach.

Grace got onto the bike and cycled fast along the road to Seal Bay.

Chapter 9

Seal Pup

The sea was splashing over the rocks, swirling into the rock pools, filling them up and refreshing them. The tide must be coming back in. Grace laid down the bike at the edge of the road, took the baby bottle out of the pannier. She wrapped the towel round it tightly. She peered down at the beach, squinting against the light. A large black-headed gull took off from the rocks, flapping away over the water as she climbed down.

Where was the pup?

Grace scanned the rocks, searching. She was sure she remembered the rock where the seal pup had been lying before. But there was no sign of it now.

In the short time she'd been away, had the mother seal swum here and nudged her baby back into the water, carried it on her back and swum away with it to safety? Or perhaps the pup had wriggled its own way down to the sea and swum away by itself.

Grace knew she should be happy; pleased for the pup. A bit of her was. But another bit wasn't. In her head, she had been making up stories about herself and the seal. She had so wanted to be the girl who helped a baby seal. She'd imagined making friends with it. They would swim in the sea together and play in the surf . . . Grace and her tame seal, famous all over the island. Col would be amazed! And now none of that could happen . . .

She sat down, still clutching the towel-wrapped bottle. In the nearest rock pool, small fish darted under a rock. As she looked up, a flicker of movement caught her eye. Her heart beat faster. Maybe it wasn't all over after all.

Yes. She could see now. It was the seal pup. It had moved, and now it lay in the shadow of a large rock, camouflaged on a bed of seaweed. It was watching her. It opened its mouth and cried at her, as if it knew she had come to help. It moved its back flippers, rocking back and forth.

'Oh!' A sudden rush of tenderness made her eyes fill with tears. The seal pup looked weaker than before; its eyes not quite so clear and shiny. Its skin was wrinkled and loose. It urgently needed to drink some milk or it really might die. Grace unwrapped the bottle. It was warm and comforting against her hand.

'It's OK. I'm coming, little seal.' Grace spoke softly all the time she picked her way down the platform of weedy rocks, between the rock pools. Slowly, she edged closer to the seal. It shrank back from her, but it still cried and stared with its beautiful eyes as if it wanted to tell her something. It was calling to her, and something in her was answering back.

Grace crouched down. She shuffled closer, little by little. She took off the cap and held the bottle out so that the soft teat pointed towards the pup. She squeezed the plastic sides so that a drip of milk dribbled onto the seaweed near the pup's head, to show it what was inside the bottle.

Was it sniffing the smell? Or simply moving its head? Grace waited, patiently. It was hard to hold the bottle still; her arms ached with holding it out for so long and her legs began to shake.

She shifted position. Now, she could easily reach out and touch the seal, but she knew that was wrong. She mustn't make the seal pup smell of her, of human, in case the mother seal came back. If her baby smelt of human, the seal mother might reject it. That happened to wild animals sometimes, Grace knew.

She held the bottle closer to the seal's mouth, nudged the teat against its muzzle.

The pup jerked its head away. She tried again. Tears came into her eyes: why did it have to be so hard? The storybook had made it sound so easy to look after a tame seal. But this seal pup didn't want to suck a bottle. It didn't know how. It was too different from sucking milk from its mother.

For a second, the seal seemed to nudge the bottle, as if it knew there was food for it somewhere close. Grace closed her eyes so she could wish extra hard. *Please suck the bottle*, she said in her head. *Please, little seal. You need to drink the milk.*

But it didn't. It couldn't. It didn't understand what to do, even though it was so hungry.

Grace shifted even closer. 'It's OK, I won't hurt you,' she whispered over and over. She dribbled some of the lukewarm milk from the bottle onto her fingers, and she held them out to the baby seal instead. But it wasn't like feeding a lamb or a kitten or a puppy; the seal pup stared and wriggled and flapped. It rocked on its front and back flippers as it tried its hardest to get away from her.

This close up, Grace saw for the first time a thin line of red on the seal pup's neck: a painful cut, as if it had been sliced by something sharp. Maybe it had been caught in a net and cut itself, struggling free? 'You poor, poor thing!' she said softly.

The pup had stopped moving. It was silent, now, as if it had given up.

I have to get help! Grace thought. *It's up to me.*

She thought hard. She remembered the poster about seals at the community centre. Hadn't there been something about stranded seals, and a telephone number for seal rescue? If only she'd written it down! But it was no use thinking like that. She needed to get a move on.

Grace looked directly at the seal pup and spoke softly to it. 'I'll be back soon. Don't give up.'

She made her plan as she scrambled back up the rocks to the road. She would cycle to the community centre; with any luck, she'd find Granny at the café. Together they would phone the rescue people. Granny would come back with her to look after the seal till they arrived . . . It would be all right, if only she could be quick enough.

Grace pedalled as fast as she could. It was hard work: she had to cycle against the wind. Little brown birds flew up from the barley fields as she went past. Two swans skidded across an inland lochan, splashing noisily as they beat their wings and took flight. She came to a fork in the road: which way was it? *Hurry up Grace!* she told herself. Both roads looked much the same, winding over the island between small fields, peat bog, heather. Grace took the right-hand turning. She went past a row of old cottages with thick stone walls and tarry black roofs. A sheep dog ran out of a yard, yipping at the bike as she cycled on. Everywhere there were birds: skylarks singing their hearts out! She knew the names of those because they were Granny's favourites.

At last she saw the Giddy Goat café sign, and the building ahead. Relief flooded through her whole body. Phew! Nearly there.

She leant the bike against the window and pushed the door open. The café was totally empty. A door was ajar at the back of the kitchen, but when she called out 'Hello' no one answered, no one came. There was no sign of Granny or her friend Angus or anyone.

Grace ran through the double doors into the community centre. The seal poster was directly ahead of her. Heart racing, she read the words at the bottom:

On no account try to help a seal pup back into the sea. It may not be able to swim and will drown.

Do not touch a seal pup. It will bite and its mouth contains bacteria which may be harmful to you. Keep well away. Keep dogs and other people away.

Leave a seal pup for 24 hours to see if its mother returns. Watch from a distance.

If the mother has not returned within 24 hours, or if the seal pup is injured, phone the number below for the marine mammal medic. (British Divers Marine Life and Rescue)

Grace found a pencil on the table next to the visitors' book. She copied the rescue number onto the back of a leaflet she found about rare birds called corncrakes. She ran back out of the centre and got on her bike again. Her legs were tired, but she had to hurry. The seal pup's life depended on her.

Chapter 10

Rescue

All the way back, Grace thought about what to say on the telephone. Perhaps Granny would be home by now; she really hoped so. Grace began to wonder where Granny could be all this time; it wasn't like her not to say she was going out. Why hadn't she left Grace a note? And why was there no one in the café or the community centre? Grace began to worry that something else was wrong, not just the seal pup.

She made herself concentrate on cycling as fast as she could.

She jumped off the bike and ran in through the front door. 'Granny?' she called.

No one answered. The house was silent and empty.

Grace fished the leaflet with the rescue number out of her pocket. Hands trembling, she dialled the number. The phone rang and rang. In her head, Grace practised what to say when they answered.

An automatic message clicked on.

'No one is available to speak to you right now. Please leave us a message. If you have found an injured marine animal, please leave us your name and number and details of what the animal is and the exact place where you found it. Do not attempt to rescue it yourself.'

Grace took a deep breath. She spoke slowly and clearly. 'I've found a seal pup stranded on the rocks and it's hurt and it's on Seal Bay. I'm Grace and this is my granny's telephone. Please come quick.' She said Granny's phone number. She put the phone back.

Now what? It was still up to her. The rescue people might take hours. She had to go back to the rocks and save her seal baby before the tide came any higher. The words from the poster kept running round her head. *It may not be able to swim and will drown . . .*

Somehow, she would have to pick up the seal pup and carry it home with her . . . wrap it up in her jumper or something . . . hope it didn't bite her. She didn't know how she was going to manage it, but she would. She was determined. Even without Granny's help.

But where was Granny? Why was she taking so long? Grace began to feel more worried.

She found a piece of paper and a pen. Quickly, she scribbled a note to tell Granny what had happened and where she was, in case she came back before Grace did. She ran back outside.

This time, she couldn't bear to get back on the bike: her legs ached too much. Instead, she jogged along the beach. The tide was much higher. Of course it was. All that time she'd been cycling to get help, the sea had been coming in steadily. She had to dodge the waves as they broke onto the sand and spread like lace. She rolled up her jeans and took off her shoes. Fear coiled in her stomach: about Granny, about the seal, about everything. Suddenly, she wished Mum and Dad were here. Even Kit. She wished she'd gone to fetch Col. But there wasn't time now.

She clambered over the rocks up to the road, and then back down the other side, onto Seal Bay. The sea had come right up over the rocks. It swirled and eddied, covering all the rock pools so completely that you'd never guess they were there.

Grace's eyes filled with tears.

She was too late.

For a few minutes she simply stared at the swirling water. Her tears made everything look fuzzy and blurred.

There was no way her seal pup could have survived, was there? It would have been washed off the rocks as the tide came in, and swept back out to sea and drowned.

It was too sad to think about it.

Unless . . .

Unless . . .

A little bubble of hope started to grow inside Grace . . .

Unless all this time, the mother seal *had* been waiting out at sea, and the moment Grace had gone, as soon as the tide was high enough, she had swum into the bay and let her baby climb onto her back and she had swum back with it to the rocks Col had told her about, on the uninhabited island.

It was perfectly possible.

Those words on the poster came back to her: *Leave a pup for 24 hours to see if its mother returns . . .*

Its mother returns . . .

As if that was what normally happened . . .

Yes. It was perfectly possible.

So she mustn't feel so sad.

She had done her best. She had done the right things. And maybe it was all going to be all right. If she sat still and watched, she might even see the seal mother with the seal pup, swimming out to the far-off rocks, the two of them safely together again.

She should have brought Granny's binoculars with her.

Grace gazed out to sea. It was so bright and sparkly she could hardly see anything. She shaded her eyes

with her cupped hands, and scanned the blue water, searching for two seal heads bobbing in the waves. She searched for ages.

Finally, Grace sat down at the top of the beach on the dry rocks. They were warm in the sun. She'd been so busy before that she'd hardly noticed that the clouds had lifted and the sun had come out. You'd never think there had been such a storm in the night. Now, it was the perfect sunny day that Granny had promised.

And yet, Grace couldn't feel happy, not while she still didn't know what had happened to her seal pup. If only things had been different, and she'd managed to bring the seal pup home, like the girl in Granny's book. She could have cuddled it, and fed it milk from the baby bottle until it was old enough to eat fish, and given it a name . . .

The baby bottle. Grace realized she had left it on the rocks, earlier, and forgotten all about it. It would have been washed out to sea long ago. She imagined the small plastic bottle bobbing on the waves, going further and further out. For some reason, the thought of it made her feel even more sad and alone.

Chapter 11

★

Col

Grace wasn't sure how long she'd been sitting there, thinking up names she could have called her baby seal. *Lora . . . Mina . . . Mara . . .* Suddenly the whole sky was filled with a weird whirring sound. She looked up. A blue helicopter came buzzing into view. For a moment, Grace wondered if it was the marine rescue people coming to look for her seal pup, responding to her telephone message. She'd have to tell them they were too late.

The sound got louder and more buzzy. It was so loud it felt as if her whole body was vibrating. She put her hands over her ears. The helicopter kept going,

straight over her head and out over the sea. Grace stared after it. She read the words on the side. *Air-sea Rescue.* Where was it going? Had something happened? She remembered what Granny had said to her, about the helicopter being for emergencies . . .

What if something had happened to Granny?

Grace stood up. She started to run.

The first thing Grace noticed as she got close to the house was Granny's bike, parked next to hers. Thank goodness! Granny must be back home, and safe. She should have noticed before that Granny had taken the bike to go somewhere.

Grace clattered up the wooden steps and into the kitchen.

Granny was standing at the table, reading her note, as if she'd only just that minute got home. 'Oh Grace! There you are. I'm sorry I've been so long. I hope you didn't worry too much.' Granny threw her arms round Grace and hugged her so tight Grace could hardly breathe. 'What's happened with the seal pup? Is it all right? I wish I'd been here to help you. Oh dear, it's been such a difficult morning.'

Grace started to cry. She couldn't stop. Now that she was safe in Granny's arms, all Grace's worry and sadness and disappointment spilt out of her in tears.

Granny understood. She held Grace tight, and smoothed her hair, and let her cry until it was all out of her. 'I'm here now,' Granny said over and over. 'It's all right, darling.'

Granny sat Grace down at the kitchen table. She listened while Grace told her everything.

'Do you think it was OK? Do you think its mother did come to fetch it home?' Grace asked Granny. 'It didn't drown, did it?'

Granny soothed her. 'It's very likely it could swim, Grace. Harbour seal pups swim almost the moment they are born. And very probably the mother seal was watching, waiting for the opportunity to rescue her pup. It happens all the time. In a few days' time we might even spot them out at sea together. We'll go and search with the binoculars later; you and me together.'

'But where were you?' Grace asked. 'Why were you so long?'

Granny looked very serious. 'I've been at Flora's house, and then round at Kate's—Col's mother. Everyone is very upset. There's been some bad news, I'm afraid. So as soon as I heard I had to go and see what I could do to help the family.'

'What news? What family? I don't understand, Granny. What's happened?'

Granny's face was grey with worry. It made Grace anxious too.

'The storm last night—you know how bad it was. Well, the *Katie May* fishing boat didn't come back to the harbour in the evening, when she should have done.

There's been no news since. The *Katie May* is Col's dad's fishing boat, Grace. Col's dad and his friend Mack are missing at sea.'

It was hard to take it in, the story Granny was now telling her about Col's dad's boat.

Granny explained. 'The *Katie May* should have returned at dusk, but by that time the storm had hit the island. There were huge waves out at sea. Everyone hoped that the boat had taken shelter somewhere else, another island perhaps. But there was no message from them last night. None this morning. The satellite system isn't working. No one has heard anything from the boat, not even the coastguard or the rescue service. No one saw any distress flares go up. There's been nothing at all to suggest what's happened.' Granny reached out for Grace's hand. 'So you see, Grace, everyone's afraid that the boat has gone down.'

Grace stared at Granny for a moment. *Gone down?* Did she mean the boat had *sunk*? 'So Col's dad might have drowned in the storm?' Grace asked. 'That's terrible!'

Granny nodded. 'But we mustn't give up hoping. There's still a chance the men are all right. Let's be as positive as we can. And we'll keep busy. That always helps.'

'I have to see Col,' Grace said. 'He's my friend.'

'Of course,' Granny said. 'It's particularly hard for Col. But right now he needs to be with his mum and his granny. Let's have some lunch, first, and then you can go to see him.'

Grace remembered her beach treasure from earlier that day. She tipped the cowrie shells onto the kitchen table.

Granny picked one up and took it to the window to see it better. 'So pretty,' she said. 'I haven't seen one of these for ages. And look how many you found! People say they bring luck. Let's hope so.'

Grace showed her the bird skull, too. 'It doesn't smell; it's been washed clean by the sea. I'm going to give it to Col, for his collection.'

The post office shop was buzzing with people as Grace cycled past. People were huddled on the road outside, talking intently, as if they were waiting for something to happen. They took no notice of her.

She went down the lane to Col's house and the harbour. The small red fishing boat she'd seen before from Col's bedroom window was tied up to the harbour wall. She could see its name painted in black along one side: *Mairi Rose*. There were other small boats, and a few people gathered at the end of the harbour wall, looking out to sea. But there was no sign of a fishing boat called *Katie May*.

Grace tried to imagine what Col must be feeling, waiting and waiting for his dad. Not knowing what had happened, or even if his dad was alive. Hoping and wishing and praying that he was safe somewhere, that good news would come soon.

Imagine if that was her dad . . .

For a moment, she thought about what it must have been like for Granny, when Grandpa was taken in the helicopter to the hospital.

She turned round, to look up at Col's house. The door was firmly shut. No one was at the window. Poor Col. She wanted to tell him how sorry she was, and that she was thinking about him, and hoping it would all have a happy ending . . .

Slowly, she walked towards the door. Her hand was shaky as she knocked.

She waited.

The door opened. Col's nan, Flora, stood there.

'Can I see Col?' Grace said. 'I came to find . . . to see if he wanted to see me . . . ' her voice drained away. 'I'm so sorry . . . '

'He's gone out on his bike,' Flora said. 'He needed some air. He's been out for a while. But thank you for calling, Grace. I'll tell him you were asking for him.'

Grace turned away. She picked the bike up again.

She wanted so much to show Col she was thinking about him. That she cared about him.

Where might he have gone?

She remembered the otter place Col liked. She could go there, first. There was no harm in trying. And if he was there, he still might not want to see her, but that would be all right, too. She'd understand.

Chapter 12

Hope

Grace got back on her bike. Overhead, seagulls were squawking and diving and making a terrible racket. They all flew off together in a sudden swoosh of wings away over the harbour wall.

As she cycled, Grace's mind darted about like a bird. *Tiny Arctic terns, that fly thousands and thousands of miles . . . sea beans washed over oceans, from a Caribbean island to here . . . Mum and Dad and Kit and the twins, hundreds of miles away . . . everything moving and changing . . . a seal pup swimming with its mother . . . Col's dad, lost at sea in a storm . . .*

She was crossing the island, trying to remember

which way she'd gone before with Col to see the otters. She found the way by instinct; gradually, she was getting to know the island for herself. Now, she could see a blue triangle of sea beyond a stretch of moorland.

This side of the island was more sheltered. The sun was hot, out of the wind. If she wasn't looking for Col, it would be nice to go all the way down to the sea and paddle or even swim. It was oddly quiet. It was as if she was the only person on the whole island . . . her island . . . as if she was a real island girl.

Grace stopped to take off her jacket. She stuffed it into one of the panniers. She wished she'd brought a drink with her. She came to a peaty stream. It looked familiar. Was this the place she and Col had left the bikes, last time? She walked a bit further, pushing the bike over the rough ground.

A bike lay half-hidden in the longer grass next to a clump of purple heather.

An old, rusty bike.

Col's bike.

Grace laid her bike on the grass next to his. There was no sign of him, yet. Of course not; he must be hiding, watching the otters.

Grace crept forwards as quietly as she could.

She found him hunched at the top of the pebbly beach, his head in his hands.

He must have heard her. He looked round, and Grace saw that his face was streaked with tears.

A little way out in the sea, something went *plop*. Col turned back. Grace followed his gaze. Bubbles rippled out over the surface, making a ring of bright water. There was another ripple and a splash and Grace saw the brown head of an otter, a silver fish thrashing in its mouth. The otter swam with the fish across the bay. A second, much smaller otter followed.

Grace quietly sat down next to Col. Neither of them said anything. They simply sat and watched as the whole otter family—mum and three cubs—fished and played among the kelp. Grace knew it was exactly the right thing to do, simply to sit quietly with Col and wait until he was ready to talk, if he wanted to. And it was fine if he didn't.

The sun was warm on their faces. The sea lapped against the pebbles, rolling them over as it sucked back.

The otters were fishing for crabs, Grace worked out. Did a baby seal eat crabs, too?

The otter family moved further along the bay, until Grace couldn't see them any longer.

She uncrossed her legs and stood up, stretching out her spine. She'd got stiff from sitting still so long.

Col seemed to look at her properly for the first time, as if he was finally taking in the fact that she was there with him.

'Dad's boat didn't come back last night,' he said, and a sob caught in his throat.

Grace nodded. 'Granny told me.' She took a deep breath. 'I'm so sorry, Col. But don't give up. You have to keep hoping.'

Col didn't say anything.

Grace sat back down. Now the otters had gone, she didn't know what to do except sit with Col. If he'd let her. She couldn't tell what he was thinking. If it was Molly, she would have hugged her and Molly would have cried. But Col was different. He didn't show his feelings in the same way.

'It was amazing, seeing your otters,' Grace said.

'They're not *my* otters,' Col said. 'They are wild animals. They don't belong to anyone but themselves.'

Grace thought about her seal pup.

Col was right.

Not *hers* at all.

Col stood up. He didn't look at Grace. 'I'm going now.'

'OK,' Grace said. She knew he didn't want her to go with him. 'I'll see you soon, Col. I'll be thinking about you.'

She waited a few minutes, to let him get ahead, and then she walked back up the path to fetch her bike. She cycled slowly up the road, following the small figure of Col way ahead of her. She'd never catch up, and she didn't mean to. He wanted to be by himself. She understood that. But it was hard, not being able to help him, or comfort him, or make a difference.

Grace was almost back, cycling along the beach road towards Granny's house. Sunlight reflected off the big windows, dazzlingly bright. It was as if the house was made of light. It filled Grace with hope.

And at the same moment, the sky was suddenly full of that whirring sound again. Grace looked up. Another blue helicopter chugged low over the island and out to sea. Three cars drove past her in quick succession. A boat engine roared somewhere over towards the harbour area, too far off for her to see. Something was happening.

She cycled on slowly, stopping each time a car came by. She'd never seen so many cars here before. It seemed that the island was suddenly alive with people. From every cottage and farm and isolated house, people were coming, some running, some driving or cycling like her, and everyone was making their way towards the harbour.

Grace kept cycling straight on past Granny's house to join them.

At last, there must be news about the *Katie May*.

Grace parked her bike at the end of the row of cottages. She walked along the lane as far as the low wall in front of Col's house at the top of the pebbly beach. She sat down to catch her breath. From here, she had a clear view of everything that was happening.

The end of the harbour wall was packed with people, all staring out to the stretch of sea beyond. An engine throbbed, as if a motorboat was coming closer. Gulls circled overhead. A cheer went up from the crowd. Grace's heart beat faster. It must be good news.

A grey inflatable boat zoomed through the gap into the harbour. A man in red overalls and a bright yellow life vest steered the boat towards the stone wall. It slowed down and spluttered to a stop at the foot of the steps. Grace watched as two other men climbed out, helped by the man in the yellow life vest. They staggered up the steep steps. The people at the top reached down to help them up.

The crowd rushed forward, hugging and crying and slapping the men on the back. One of the men bent down and picked up a child and put him on his shoulders. Benny! And there was Kate, rushing forward.

So, the man with the dark hair and a tanned face in blue overalls must be Col's dad. He was safe. Grace felt relief flood through her. She watched as he hugged Kate and baby Lewis. Col's nan Flora was hugging them all, now.

Grace spotted Angus from the café . . . and was that Granny, next to Angus? The whole island community had come to welcome home the missing men.

Grace watched it all from her place, sitting on the wall.

But where was Col? She couldn't see him anywhere. His dad was safely home, and maybe he still didn't know . . .

She wished she knew where to find Col. She could be the one to tell him the wonderful news.

Grace slid down from the wall and walked along

the lane towards the churchyard. Her feet took her straight to Grandpa's grave. She simply needed to be close to him. Swallows swooped through the air, catching midges. Grace could almost hear Grandpa's voice, telling her that swallows come back to nest at the same place every summer. They spend the winter in Africa, and they fly thousands of miles back to the place they were born. *Like your granny*, he'd told her. *She had to come back to the island where she was born and where she belongs. And so I had to come too, because I love her, and her happiness makes mine.*

Grace sat down on the grass. It was comforting and peaceful here; the only sounds were the whispering of the grass, the sound of the sea and the twittering voices of the swallows. A fat bumblebee buzzed over the grave.

A new sound came: tyres on tarmac. A bike was whizzing along. Grace heard the squeak of rusty brakes and the skid of a wheel on dry ground and looked up.

Col had stopped at the churchyard gate: on his face was a look of total joy as he saw the crowd of people on the harbour wall and heard the voices. He didn't notice Grace. He was already pedalling on, fast as he could, ready to meet his dad.

Chapter 13

★

Sunset

Now it was evening. From the decking, Grace watched a small figure running along the beach, swerving in and out as if he was driving a racing car or flying a plane. It could only be one person, but even so, she fetched Granny's binoculars and watched Col's progress along the sand. It made her heart turn over to see him so full of happiness.

He waved at her and she waved back.

He changed track, and jogged up towards the house. He clattered up the wooden steps, still smiling.

'Dad's back safe!' Col said.

'It's brilliant!' Grace said. She stood up and hugged Col before she realized what she was doing.

Col didn't seem to mind too much. He flopped down on one of the chairs. 'The boat got blown off course in the storm, and the engine failed, and all the technical equipment went down. They drifted for hours and finally they managed to get themselves into the shelter of a tiny rocky island, but they had no way of letting us know they were safe.'

'It must have been terrible, waiting,' Grace said.

'Mum was in a right state,' Col said.

'Yes.'

'She always thinks the worst.'

Grace didn't say anything.

'Anyway, there's going to be a big party, and you're invited.' Col grinned.

'What, now? Tonight?'

Granny came out to join them. 'What's happening tonight?'

'Nothing,' Col said. 'But tomorrow there's a ceilidh at the community centre and everyone's invited.'

'That's great,' Granny said. 'A proper celebration. We'll both come, won't we Grace?'

'Yes!'

The sun was going down over the sea, making a path of gold over the water. The sky was full of colour: streaks of pink and apricot and turquoise fading to pale blue and purple. It was well after Grace's usual bedtime, but because there was still so much light it didn't feel late.

'Isn't it beautiful?' Granny said. 'The most beautiful place on earth! Where else can you get skies like these?' She looked at Col. 'I'm so very happy about your dad, Col. That's the best news ever.'

'I saw the helicopters,' Grace said to Col. 'Was it them who found your dad?'

Col nodded. 'The air-sea rescue helicopter finally spotted the *Katie May*. They'd been searching all day. They had to send a RIB to bring Dad and Mack home because there was nowhere to land a helicopter and it was too tricky to do a rescue from the air.'

'What's a RIB?' Grace asked.

'A rigid inflatable boat,' Granny explained.

'The *Katie May* still has to be towed back,' Col said. 'She'll need a lot of repair work. New engine and satellite and everything. It'll cost loads. Dad won't be able to fish for months.'

'One thing at a time,' Granny said. 'Let's just be thankful that they're safely home.'

Col got up from the chair, as if he was too full of excitement to stay still for long. 'Got to go. I'll see you tomorrow night,' he said to Grace.

She watched him zig-zag back the way he'd come. His feet left prints in the damp sand: a track, following him home.

'Come inside before the midges get you, Grace!' Granny slapped at the tiny dark insects on her bare arms. 'That's what happens when the wind drops. But tomorrow will be a beautiful day: a swimming-and-picnic day. Red sky at night, fisherman's delight!'

'Shepherd's, not fisherman's!' Grace said. 'And it's not red, Granny; it's pink, and orange, and green, and blue.'

Granny laughed. 'And now it's time for a bath and bed,' she said. 'I'm tired, even if you aren't!'

When Grace had got ready for bed, Granny came in to say goodnight. She sat at the foot of Grace's bed. She leant forwards, and stroked Grace's cheek gently. 'Your face has caught the sun today. We need to be more careful. Please remember to wear your sun hat tomorrow.'

Grace yawned. She was tired, after all. 'Are there any stories about baby Selkies?' she asked.

'Some people think that Selkies are the souls of people lost at sea. I suppose some of them might be children. And there are stories about babies being found washed up on rocks, cradled in the seaweed. Once upon a time, an island woman who couldn't have a child of her own was walking along the shore, and she found a baby like that, sleeping on the seaweed on the rocks, and brought her home and cared for her, fed her milk from a bottle, and knitted her warm clothes spun from sheep's wool. The baby grew into a beautiful girl with golden hair, who loved the sea and swam like a seal . . . ' Granny was quiet for a while. 'Are you thinking about the stranded seal pup, Grace?'

Grace nodded. 'The pup was wounded on its neck, as if it had been caught in a net.'

'A small cut will heal in time. If it was very badly injured, nature would simply take her course,' Granny said gently. 'A badly injured seal won't be able to catch fish so it can't survive for long. That's nature's way. It's not for us to interfere. That's just how it is, Grace. Life and death, all part of the way things are. But I reckon your seal pup will be getting better now it's back with its mother.'

'If it is. We still don't know, for sure.' Grace turned her face towards the pillow and shut her eyes tight.

Granny sat there for a while. She leant forward and stroked Grace's hair.

'Be happy for Col, tonight,' Granny said. 'Imagine how differently that story might have ended, Grace. Thank goodness that one had a happy outcome.'

Grace kept her eyes shut, and stayed still, so Granny would think she was already asleep. She didn't want Granny to see the tears pooling onto her pillow. Of course she was happy for Col and his family. But it didn't stop her feeling sad that she couldn't save the seal pup. She'd tried so hard.

Finally, Granny tiptoed out and softly closed the bedroom door behind her.

Grace dreamt she was in deep water, tumbled over by waves, struggling to hold her head up to breathe. It was dark. She was gasping for air, pressure building in her lungs, too exhausted to swim any longer.

Something solid nudged her from beneath; her hands felt furry skin. A fully grown seal lifted her up and held her above the waves so she could take a shuddering breath. She held on tight as the seal swam with her on its back and carried her to the shore.

She lay on her back on the sand, taking deep breaths of cold air. Above her, the night sky was a blanket stitched with a million stars.

Grace woke in darkness. She listened to the soft murmur of calm sea. She reached out and pulled the curtains apart. The moon was shining so bright and silver it lit up the beach and made a silver path across the water. She strained her eyes searching for seals, longing for the sight of a small seal carried on the back of its mother. She wanted to see it so much she almost imagined she did. Was that the dark head of a seal, riding the surf, with another, smaller one close behind?

Grace climbed out of bed. She padded across the bedroom and into the living room. She found the binoculars on the window seat and took them back with her. She sat on the edge of her bed, focused the binoculars and scanned the sea.

There were two seals swimming in the bay. As she watched, they swam right in, close to the shore. They lifted their heads. They seemed to be looking straight back at her. A mother seal and a young one, both pale in the moonlight.

Grace opened the window wide. She looked again with the binoculars. She could see their faces clear as anything. The dark eyes, the whiskers, the soft mouth that looked like a smile.

She craned forwards: what was that she could hear?

A strange and magical sound wafted towards her on the air, like voices carried on the wind. Two seals were singing to her, calling her name.

And then both seals dived, and disappeared.

Grace curled back under the duvet, leaving the curtains open so the silvery light shone onto her bed and filled the room with its magic. It lit up the little driftwood boat with its white cotton sail; the mother-of-pearl shell; Grace's drawing, and the sea-washed bird skull she would give to Col. It played over the sea-coloured skirt draped over the chair.

Grace slept, her face bathed in moonlight, her heart full of joy.

Chapter 14

★

Island Girl

Tonight was the party. Grace was excited. It seemed too long to have to wait all day. But it was a perfect day for swimming, Granny said. 'We'll go to a little beach where I used to swim when I was a child. We'll take a picnic and our swimming things.'

Grace and Granny cycled side by side across the island. The beach was a long ride away, on the north-west of the island. Grace had never been this way before. They came over the brow of a small hill and saw below them a sheltered cove: the bluest sea spangled with sunlight. Small waves washed onto silver sand. In the centre of the beach a shallow stream wound down to the sea, cutting a channel through the sand.

'Wow!' Grace said. 'It's perfect, like a postcard picture.'

'It's my idea of paradise,' Granny said.

Paradise was not a word Grace had ever heard before. But she liked the sound of it.

Grace changed into her swimsuit: turquoise, with green seahorses. She shivered: it was still too early in the morning to be really hot. She put on her baggy jumper over her swimsuit, shoved on her sunhat and ran down to join Granny. The sand was deliciously firm under her feet. She danced round and did a cart-wheel before wading across the shallow stream to where Granny was bending down to pick up shells.

'See these?' Granny said. 'These are cockle shells. When I was your age, I used to collect cockles and we cooked and ate them.' She gave one of the white shells to Grace to show her.

'Can I swim now?' Grace asked.

'Of course! I'll come in too. It'll be cold, mind. It never really warms up, even in summer.'

Grace danced back up the beach to take off her jumper and sunhat, and Granny followed more slowly.

'Race you in!' Grace called, already running down to the sea. She ran straight in, splashing and shrieking as the cold got up to her knees, and her thighs and her middle and then she plunged in properly and began to swim in her usual breaststroke that she'd learnt with school. Next she tried crawl, and back stroke, and butterfly. The water felt soft, like silk.

She stopped swimming and flipped over on to her back, and floated, bobbing over each small wave as it came and lifted her and carried on, sweeping into the shore. Above her, the sky curved like a blue bowl. She spread out her arms and legs to make the shape of a star and floated like that. She flipped over again, to swim towards Granny.

'You swim like a seal!' Granny said. 'You're very good at it, Grace.' Granny swam alongside Grace for a while but she didn't stay in long. 'Too cold for me!' she said.

'Your lips have gone blue!' Grace said.

Later, they lay on the sand and warmed up in the sun. They shared the picnic.

'I should go back soon and get on with a few things,' Granny said. 'But you can stay as long as you like, Grace. Don't swim, though. Not without me here to keep an eye on you.'

A family with three small children came tumbling down the sandy path at the top of the beach. Grace watched them set up camp with stripy windbreaks and big towels and a cool box. Two of the children ran down to make dams in the stream.

'That's exactly what Kit would do, if he was here,' Grace said.

'Are you missing him?' Granny asked.

'Only a bit.'

The dad unpacked a kite and took the little girl with him to fly it above the sweep of silver sand. The mum settled herself in a deckchair with a book.

'I'll go back now. See you later. Allow enough

time to get home and ready for the party,' Granny said. 'You'll remember the way back?'

Grace nodded. 'It's not difficult. The island's too small for me to get lost. And I can always ask someone.'

The air was warming up fast. She put on her sun-hat and rubbed suncream onto her bare skin. She dozed in the sun, happy and tired after the swimming and picnic. She watched the family nearby get their picnic lunch out of the cool box and eat it under a blue sunshade the mum put up.

The little girl wandered over to Grace and stared at her with solemn eyes while she munched a sandy sandwich.

'Hello!' Grace said.

The girl watched Grace but didn't speak.

Grace sifted dry sand through her fingers. The little girl squatted down and tried to do the same. She dropped her sandwich in the sand and stared at it, but she didn't cry.

'Shall we make a castle?' Grace asked.

The little girl nodded.

Grace stood up, and walked slowly over to the wet sand near the stream. The girl followed. Grace showed her how to make a fairy castle with turrets by trickling wet sand slowly through her fingers. It was the sort of thing she'd do with Kit.

The little girl laughed and clapped her hands.

The mum came over to take a photo. 'It's perfectly lovely!' she said to Grace. 'Thanks for playing with Jas.'

Grace smiled. 'That's OK. It's fun.'

'I can tell you're used to little children,' the woman said.

'I've got a little brother and twin baby sisters,' Grace explained. 'But they're at home.'

'Lucky you, living on this lovely island. It must be amazing!'

Grace didn't tell her that she didn't, that her real home was hundreds of miles away, that she was just a visitor. It was nice, for a little while, pretending that she really was an island girl.

Chapter 15

Party-time at the Giddy Goat

Seal Bay was like a magnet, drawing her towards it. Grace was nearly back at Granny's: she was at the turning onto the beach road. All she had to do was cycle left for a short distance and she'd be home. But at the last minute, Grace went the other way. She couldn't resist.

It was a shock to see people on the beach. Families with children; old people with deckchairs; a group of teenagers with bodyboards and wetsuits. She'd never seen Seal Bay so busy. There were cars parked along the edge of the road, people shaking sand out of their shoes before they got in. Doors slammed and engines started up. It didn't feel like her beach anymore. Not a beach for seals, either.

But people were packing up and leaving now the tide was coming up and it was teatime. Grace left her bike on the grass and sat down on the rocks to wait for them all to go.

The last car drove off. Gulls swooped down on the strip of beach to pick up bits of picnic left behind. Almost as if they had all been waiting too, flocks of small brown birds flew in low over the sea and landed at the water's edge. They ran in and out of the waves making a peeping sound. Now it was quiet, except for the lapping waves and the seabirds. Grace peered at the sea, hoping and wishing so hard for a sign of a seal.

And at last: one small rounded head, bobbing up, disappearing, reappearing a bit closer in. A seal. The water was so clear she could see the way its body moved and turned as it swam. The seal dived again.

'Seal!' Grace called. 'Where are you? Come back.' She waited for ages without seeing anything. She tried to think of a song to sing: a seal-summoning song. She suddenly remembered Grandpa singing to her when she was little. The words came to her, as if she had always known them: '*Speed bonny boat like a bird on the wing, over the sea . . .*'

Like magic, the seal's head bobbed up. It had come back, and it was listening.

Grace held her breath. Might there be a second, smaller seal about to join its mother? She remembered last night; it was all hazy, now, a bit like a dream. The two seals, and the sound, like singing, drifting across the sand on the night air . . .

This seal swam closer, dived and re-surfaced. It was so close she could see its big eyes, its whiskery nose. She sat and sang, hoping so much to summon a pup with her song, but there was only the one seal, listening and watching her, almost as if it wanted to speak to her.

Little by little, singing Grandpa's song made Grace feel as if he was sitting close beside her, calming her, telling her that everything was all right, just as it should be.

The light changed as afternoon turned to evening. Shadows lengthened. The sun was golden, making the sea look like liquid metal. Grace watched until the seal dived one last time and swam back out to sea.

It must nearly be time to get ready for the party.

Tonight, for the first time, she would wear the beautiful new skirt that Granny had made her.

From a distance, Grace and Granny could see the community centre lit up with coloured lights. As they got closer, they heard music. Grace's heart beat fast with excitement.

They left their bikes outside and went through the front entrance to the café. It was buzzing with people. The double doors between the café and the community centre had been propped wide open to make more space, and all the posters and display boards had been stacked away to make room for dancing. People were laughing and chatting. Granny seemed to know everyone.

'Hello, you two! Welcome!' Angus came forward and put his arms right round Granny and kissed her.

Grace hoped he wasn't going to kiss her too. But he shook her hand instead, and admired her skirt. 'You've got a bit of colour in your cheeks now!' he said. He turned back to Granny. 'Island life suits her, Mairi. And your home cooking, no doubt!'

A young man with curly dark hair was organizing everyone for the first dance. The islanders knew all the dances, but the visitors and holiday makers might not, so the caller's job was to shout out what to do at each stage of the dance. 'Join hands. Make a big circle. Skip to the right for eight steps . . . '

The ceilidh band started to play the music. The musicians were all young people: Grace recognized the accordion player as one of the wetsuited teenagers on the beach that afternoon. The girl playing the fiddle had beautiful dark hair and a red dress. She laughed a lot and her eyes danced with the music. Grace watched her. *When I'm older, I'd like to be able to play music like that*, she thought.

The room was hot and stuffy. Everyone was dancing, whatever age they were, even the men who were fishermen or farmers. It looked fun; nothing like the dancing Grace had to do at school sometimes. The island women wore special black dancing shoes with laces, and even the old women like Granny danced as lightly as if they were Grace's age. She recognized Col's mum, Kate. In her best clothes and without the children she looked different; younger and happier. She held onto Col's dad's arm tight as if she wanted to keep him safe by her side for ever.

The first dance was over. People surged over to the bar to get drinks. The caller announced the second dance: 'Now, get yourselves into circles of eight,' he said. 'Everyone join in for this one: it's easy.'

Col pushed through the crowd towards Grace. He looked different too. He'd flattened his hair down and put on a shirt.

'Come and join us,' Col said.

'I don't know the steps,' Grace said.

'You'll pick it up soon enough,' Col said. 'And it doesn't matter if you do it wrong.'

'Circle to the right, circle to the left. Into the middle and clap!' the caller shouted over the fiddle music. Soon Grace forgot to be shy. She was caught up with the dance and the music and the feeling of being part of something wonderful: a celebration of life and living, family and friendship. Her feet picked up the rhythm as if they had done this all her life.

'You're a natural!' Col's mum said. 'It's in your blood, Grace.'

'I'm thirsty,' Grace told Col, as soon as that dance was over. She pushed through the people at the bar and found a jug of orange juice, and she filled up a plastic cup for herself and one for Col.

Angus and two older ladies were taking the cling-film off plates of food: sandwiches, flans, pizzas cut into triangles, samosas, bowls of salad, and fresh French bread. 'Are you hungry, pet?' one lady asked Grace. 'Help yourself. There's plenty here.'

Col elbowed his way next to her. He piled a paper plate with food and together they took their supper out onto the terrace at the back of the centre. 'This way we miss the speeches,' he said. 'They'll go and on, you know? Like grown-ups do.'

Grace laughed. 'Why are there speeches at a dance?'

'To thank everyone for their support. A collection for the air-sea rescue fund. But any excuse, really, the island elders like to get up and make speeches.'

Grace and Col sat together on the wall, facing out over the fields of ripening barley.

'You can see sea all round, in every direction,' Grace said. 'We are right at the middle of the island.'

'The middle of everything,' Col said.

They sat together in silence for a while, eating.

'Yesterday,' Grace said, 'I found a seal pup on the rocks at Seal Bay.'

Col looked at her.

'It was stranded. Much too small to be alone. I tried

so hard to help it. I phoned the marine animal rescue number. I tried to give it some milk from a bottle, but it wouldn't suck it. It was hurt; a cut on its neck. And then, I think the sea must have washed it off the rocks when the tide came in, when I wasn't there.'

'It could probably still swim,' Col said. 'It was probably all right.'

Grace nodded. 'That's what Granny said, too.'

She didn't tell Col about the seals, singing in the moonlight. Now, she was beginning to wonder if it had happened at all. She wasn't sure that Col would believe her, anyway.

Col was quiet. Eventually he spoke. 'We could go over to see the seal pups on one of the uninhabited islands, if you like. We could row over there, if your gran will let you come.'

'Thanks, Col,' Grace said. 'I'd love that.'

It was beginning to get dark. The stars were coming out. Here, where there was so little light from houses or streets to interfere, the night skies were amazing.

'That's Venus, the evening star.' Col pointed. 'Well, it's actually a planet, not a star.'

'And there's the Plough. The North Star at the top.' Grace smiled.

Col looked surprised that she knew.

Grace laughed. 'Dad's got this app on his phone,' she explained. 'It's a brilliant way of learning the names of the stars.'

'What's that one, then?' Col pointed to a tiny pin-prick of light.

'I don't know.'

'Me neither!'

They both laughed.

Grace looked at Col. 'The music's started again. The speeches must be over.'

'Guess so.'

'Shall we go back to the party?'

'Yes.'

They walked back inside. A dance was in full swing; Grace watched Angus holding Granny's arm and dancing her through an archway made by two people at the top of the set. Granny looked happy. Grace was glad for her.

Col's dad swung Col's mum so fast her feet lifted off the ground. Her hair was coming undone and her face was pink with pleasure.

'Where are Benny and the baby?' Grace asked Col.

'Somewhere around. My nan and Auntie May are taking turns to look after them.'

Grace wished her family were here too, all of them, joining in.

She thought about her time on the island. She'd had an amazing time. She'd done so many new things. She'd seen seals; she had got really close to a small seal pup. She'd even heard seals singing, like in Granny's stories.

Maybe, Grace thought, the nicest thing of all was that she had made a new best friend. She knew she and Col would be friends for ever. She had another few days of swimming and sunbathing; a trip to see baby seals and a walk under the stars with Col. Then, *maybe*, she'd be ready to go home, back to Mum and Dad, Kit, and the babies. Molly, her best friend, would be waiting to hear everything. And next summer, of course, she could come back to the island again.

'Everyone hold hands in a big circle,' the caller announced. 'This is usually a wedding dance, with the couple in the middle. But tonight it's a dance for Jamie and Mack.'

Kate went with Jamie into the middle of the circle. Mack and his wife stepped in too. Grace and Col took their place in the circle around them and joined hands. The accordion started playing the tune. Granny took Grace's other hand, and the circle was complete.

'Having fun, Grace darling?' Granny asked.

Grace nodded. For a moment she was too full of happiness to speak. She squeezed Granny's hand tight. 'Grandpa would be pleased, to see us like this.'

'Pleased as anything. Proud of us both,' Granny said.

'I thought of a name for the little boat I made,' Grace said. 'I'm going to write it on the side, like Grandpa used to do. I'm going to call her *Island Girl*.'

'Perfect,' Granny said.

Grace watched as the girl with the red dress lifted the fiddle and settled her chin on the rest. She drew the bow across the strings, and the pure high notes spun out across the crowded room like magic. Everyone went quiet.

There was no more need for words, now. It was time to dance.

Author photograph © Kim Green

Julia Green says:

'Some of my happiest times have been spent on islands, and on beaches collecting shells and pebbles and things left by the tide. One day I'd love to live in a house like Granny's, close to the beach and with a view of seals and birds, with a peat stove to keep me warm, and shelves of books to read.

At the moment, I live on the edge of a city called Bath: I love that, too. Our garden is visited by deer, foxes, and badgers. You can read about a fox in my book, *Tilly's Moonlight Fox*, and about a girl who wants a puppy, in *Sylvie and Star*. We don't have a dog, but we do have two cats. I work at Bath Spa University, helping other people to write stories and get them published. Some of my former students are also published by Oxford University Press, including Gill Lewis and Che Golden. I love visiting schools and festivals and leading writing workshops for people of all ages.'

You can find out more about Julia by going to her website: **www.julia-green.co.uk.**

More amazing animal stories from Julia Green

'The fox called again. Its eerie cry echoed into the night. The sound wove in and out of the night garden, and into Tilly's dreams.'

When Tilly moves to a big, old house with her mum and dad, she can't wait to start exploring. There, deep in the garden, she finds a mysterious, hidden gate . . .

Led by a wild fox, Tilly discovers the magical secret that lies beyond the gate and nothing is ever quite the same again.

'The puppy would fit on one hand, it was so small. Its fur was a pale silver-grey all over, except for one dark star on its head.'

Sylvie can't wait for the school holidays so she can get back to her grandparents' farm in Italy. Their dog, Bella, is going to have puppies and Sylvie is determined to be there when they are born. Perhaps her mum and dad will even let her keep one?

There is just one puppy in the end—a tiny, furry bundle that Sylvie names Star. It soon becomes clear to everyone that there is something extra special about him—something no one was expecting.

Turn the page to read the first chapter of Sylvie and Star

Chapter 1

London: May

Sylvie half-walked, half-ran along the pavement on her way home from school, taking care not to step on the joins between the paving slabs. The words of a song jiggled round her head in time with her feet: *Don't step on the cracks, only on the squares, or you'll get taken by the bears . . .*

She ran past JJ's hair salon, past the Fat Friar fish and chip shop and the Express supermarket. She paused to catch her breath at the old-fashioned fruit-'n'-veg shop. Cauliflowers and aubergines, sweet potatoes, bananas, and mangos were piled outside on a table covered with pretend green-grass matting.

The nearest *real* green grass was a mile away, at the park, and it wasn't very green even there—patches of mud and yellowing grass where boys kicked footballs and teenagers swung and smoked on the swings, looking bored.

Sylvie started running again and kept going until she got to the traffic lights. She stopped to wait for the lights to change so she could cross the road. She looked up. High above the shops and office blocks that lined both sides of the street she could see a slice of pale blue sky. Sunlight glinted off the plate-glass office windows. Down here at pavement level you'd hardly know it was a sunny afternoon. Cars and lorries belched out diesel fumes. An empty plastic bag got sucked up in the after-draught of a passing bus, and whirled into the air for a few seconds, flapping like a wounded bird.

I hate it here! Sylvie thought fiercely.

But it was nearly the May holiday: just one more school day to go. And holidays meant *Italy*, and Nonna and Gramps's house in the middle of fields and woods with mountains all around and a silence so deep and beautiful that Sylvie could almost cry at the thought of it. All that, and Bella.

Bella was Nonna and Gramps's dog: a German Shepherd cross with silky fur: a mix of black and silver-grey and squirrel brown. She had brown eyes and pointed ears and the gentlest face. When Sylvie stayed at Nonna and Gramps's house, Bella hardly left her side. She padded after her round the garden. She walked with her over the fields and up through the trees in the forest . . .

The lights changed. Sylvie crossed with everyone else: a crush of people all scurrying home from shopping or school or work.

It was the thing Sylvie wanted more than anything, a dog of her own. But you can't keep a dog if you live in a flat, in a city, and your mum and dad are out at work all day. *It's not fair on the dog,* Mum said every time Sylvie asked.

It's not fair on me, either, Sylvie thought.

She turned off the main road, went down the tree-lined street with its large houses on either side. The trees had overgrown the circles of ground they'd been planted in years ago; their roots had pushed up and spread and made the tarmac buckle and crack. Poor trees! Did it hurt, pushing their roots up against the hard pavement?

Nearly there, now. She hurried down another smaller street where the houses were all joined together in terraces. Four red doors in a row, then a cut through to the estate and the blocks of flats where Sylvie lived with Mum and Dad, three staircases up.

She checked who was hanging about today. Mr Patel from the ground floor flat was putting a small bag of rubbish into one of the big green wheelie bins. He waved at her. She waved back. She pushed the heavy door to the stairwell and started to climb. Twelve steps to the first landing. Then another twelve. And twelve more. There was her blue front door. She was home.

She smelt onions and garlic the minute she opened the door. Mum must be back from work already. Good. Sometimes she was late on Thursdays—staff meetings, after-school clubs, whatever. Mum was a teacher at a comprehensive school. The same school where Sylvie would go in just over a year.

'Hi, Mum!'

'*Ciao, bambina!*' Mum's cheeks were flushed. She was stirring tomato and basil sauce at the stove. 'Good day at school? What did you do today?'

'Nothing much,' Sylvie said, the same as she always did after a school day. 'I'm just going to change.'

Taking off school uniform was like stepping out of the wrong skin and becoming *her* again. The real Sylvie. She pulled on jeans and a T-shirt. She undid her hair so it tumbled down her back, messy and comfortable. She went back into the kitchen and sat down at the table.

'There's a postcard for you,' Mum said, moving a pile of books out of the way.

Sylvie picked it up. The picture was a photo of the medieval bridge over the river Serchio. She turned it over.

We are looking forward to seeing you!
We will be waiting at Pisa airport.
Bella is getting excited about all the long walks
she'll have when you're here.
Sunny and hot today. 30°C.

Love
Nonna and Gramps.

'You could start packing,' Mum said. 'Just a small bag this time, seeing it's only for one week. Then we can take it as hand luggage and that will speed things up at the airport.'

Something began to unwind, deep inside Sylvie. Two days to go. She went to the living room window at the front of the flat and opened it wide. The sounds of the city drifted up: traffic, sirens, the constant roar that never stopped, even at night. Far above her, a silver streak of an aeroplane climbed up into the blue sky. Hard to imagine the people inside, it looked so tiny. That would be Mum and her, in two days' time. The happy, excited feeling bubbling up inside her made her feet want to dance.